THE DUKE'S GODDESS

Duke Dare, Book 2

Eliana Piers

ARE YOU SIGNED UP FOR DRAGONBLADE'S BLOG?

You'll get the latest news and information on exclusive giveaways, exclusive excerpts, coming releases, sales, free books, cover reveals and more.

Check out our complete list of authors, too!

No spam, no junk. That's a promise!

Sign Up Here

www.dragonbladepublishing.com

Dearest Reader;

Thank you for your support of a small press. At Dragonblade Publishing, we strive to bring you the highest quality Historical Romance from some of the best authors in the business. Without your support, there is no 'us', so we sincerely hope you adore these stories and find some new favorite authors along the way.

Happy Reading!

CEO, Dragonblade Publishing

Additional Dragonblade books by Author Eliana Piers

Duke Dare Series
The Duke's Spinster (Book 1)
The Duke's Goddess (Book 2)

CHAPTER ONE

*"Sometimes the most courageous act is simply to be yourself in
a world that wants you to be someone else."*
—Joan of Arc

1816 England

THOUGH SHE WAS quiet, she was fierce. Lady Joan was the calm, cautious, committed sister in a pack of four. It was easy to hold her tongue and let others live their lives, face the consequences of their own decisions, learn from their mistakes. If asked, she would give her opinion. But only in extreme situations did she ever offer unsolicited advice. She loved to offer support with a kind word or touch. But there was more to her than being the quiet one. There was something deep within her...just simmering. Not that she recognized it yet. Right now, she felt as though the world was (mostly) working in her favor. She had a loving family with three beautiful sisters, all of whom were currently having tea together.

"Are you excited, Bodi?" Mimi asked with shooting stars in her eyes.

"Yes, Mimi. I'm excited. For the fifth time." Bodi shook her head at the youngest, and Joan knew the feigned exasperation was all in love.

"It's. Your. Wedding. Bodi." As if none of the sisters knew what Mimi was talking about.

They all sat on Boudicca's bed, savoring the last night as four single women. Tomorrow Bodi would marry and everything would change. Thankfully the sisters were celebrating, since Bodi was marrying the man she loved, and all because of a dare. A dare that was sitting heavily on Joan's chest. Almost as heavily as she might expect from an elephant.

The duke dare...ah...that silly little, vexing, agreement. An agreement that bound her to her sisters. An agreement that she would never back out of, but really, if she had a choice, she would go back in time and let the other three pursue it and leave herself out of it. She was happy to observe. Even cheer them on. But actively participate? She wished to renege. But she wouldn't. She would go along to keep their relationship strong.

But tonight was not a night for woes, rather wonder. A wedding full of joy and warmth would envelop them tomorrow.

"I know." Bodi eyed Mimi as if to put an end to the incessant questions, but then a smile broke free on her lips. "I know. You're right. And I am thrilled to be marrying the man I love."

"Oooooh. You really love him," Mimi teased.

"We already knew that she loved him, Mimi," Nobi jumped in.

"I'm still shocked that he loves me," Bodi spoke with dreamy eyes, very much unlike her pragmatic default.

"Of course he loves you. How could he not? What's not to love?" Joan asked.

"Exactly. You're a rapier-wielding, championship-stealing, business-building beautiful soul." Mimi smiled, showing all her teeth.

"Please tell me that's not how you smile at the gentlemen, Mimi," Bodi scolded.

Mimi scoffed. "Chastised? After I said all those nice things about you?" She crossed her arms and puffed out her chest. The dynamic between the eldest and the youngest was in full force this evening.

And Joan could already predict what Nobi—the peacekeeper—would do.

"This is no time for an affectation of umbrage. Live up to

your namesake, Artemisia."

Mimi stuck her tongue out at Nobi, and Joan had to stifle a giggle.

"Tomorrow shall prove to be the best day of our lives. The first one of us is getting married. Let's focus on that," Joan said once she had her chuckles under control.

"I'm glad you're all so happy for me. Your best days are still to come. Yours might be next, Joan," Bodi said while giving Joan's forearm a squeeze.

"I'm not so sure about that," Joan let her gaze fall to the floor, following the pattern of the Aubusson rug. There might come a day when she had to marry...a duke no less—because of the dare—but she doubted that she would find true love in that venture. But if she had to accept a loveless marriage in order to keep her sisters satisfied, she would do it. Of course, if she could marry a duke for love, that was the first option. But she just couldn't envision that happening. Who was she to attract the attention of a powerful man? She was the often overlooked quiet third sister. She was a woman just eccentric enough to be talked about by some, and not scandalous enough to be rejected by society. Playing it safe was how she made her way through life. This dare was anything but safe...

"Wait." Mimi redirected her attack (albeit a mild one) to Nobi. "It should be Nobi's turn to go next, shouldn't it? She's the second eldest."

Flustered, Nobi spoke up, "We didn't establish an order for who would complete the dares at what time."

"Then why did I go first?" Bodi asked, sitting upright on the bed.

"Are you complaining?" Mimi asked.

"No, just curious."

"Well, it's simple. It's because you're our leader. We follow you. You're the oldest," Nobi replied.

"In that case, you should be next Nobi." Bodi pointed firmly to Zenobia.

"Well...erm...that is to say...I'm not sure I'm the best candidate." A flush had flanked Nobi's terse lips and she grabbed a pillow from the head of the bed. Clutching it to her chest, almost as if she were hiding behind it, she blinked hard a couple of times in wait.

"Why is that?" Mimi asked.

"I'm just not ready yet." Nobi's grasp on the pillow tightened. She twisted the corners in the opposite direction and Joan thought the pillow might pop. Though, between the pillow and Nobi, she wasn't sure which might explode first, especially since Mimi was not letting up on the questions.

"I'm going to need more than that to satisfy my questions." Case in point.

Nobi's hands flew to her face still gripping the pillow, and for a second Joan thought she might break down into tears.

"It's Christopher." She inhaled deeply. "I can't just walk up to my best friend and say I love you."

"Yes, you could actually."

Of course, Mimi would say that. She was the brash one. If she wanted to say something, she just did it. Perhaps because she was the youngest and laughed at the idea of consequences.

"I can't, Mimi. It's not that simple. What if he says no?" Joan watched the tension laced in Nobi's eyes. Her eyebrows were drawn together. Her lips were tight. And the crinkles in the corner of her eyes were cast downward.

"Well, he wouldn't say no in response to what you just said. It's not as if you'll say,"—Mimi's voice took on a high-pitched almost mocking tone—"*Ooooh Chris, I love you. I always have and always will.* And then he'll just say,"—and then her tone dropped an octave for one word—"*no.* Don't be ridiculous, Nobi."

"I'm not being ridiculous, Mimi. You are. He might not feel the same way, and then I'd be devastated. I can't lose him."

"You'd rather have him as a friend than a lover?" Mimi pushed.

The red in Nobi's cheeks darkened. "Yes."

Mimi propped her hands on her hips and glared at Nobi. "You're telling me right now that you would rather be friends with Chris, for a few years at most, until he marries someone else and then you lose him as a friend all together?" She stuck her finger in the air to cut off Nobi's protests. "And in all that short time, you prefer never having been intimate with him? Not even once. Not one single kiss."

"Mimi!" Bodi scolded for the second time in their gathering.

Mimi turned to her eldest sister. "Bodi, I'm the only one willing to tell her the truth. To paint a realistic picture for her. She needs to know what she'll be losing."

In a timid voice, Nobi spoke up, "We could still be friends."

"Pfft. Nobi. Please be honest with us. We're your sisters." Mimi threw her hands up in the air when Nobi remained silent. "If you're not going to be honest with us, then be honest with yourself. You cannot be his friend when he marries and starts having children. He's a good man. Whomever he marries will be his best friend. There will be no place in his life for a female best friend who is not related to him."

Joan would normally allow her sisters to discuss and come to their own conclusions, but seeing the tears brimming at Nobi's eyes, she had to say something. "You've said your piece, Mimi. Let Zenobia think about it now. She's already agreed to the dare, as we all have. Maybe she just needs more time." And then Joan turned to her sister and caught a small nod from Nobi.

"That just means you're next then, Joan," Mimi announced.

Right. That. Why had she agreed to the asinine duke dare again? Oh, yes. Because she wanted everyone around her to be happy. She wanted to see her sisters succeed in life. Land a duke. That sounded like the best possible plan for each of them. Mostly because it ensured that Nobi finally took her chance with Chris. It would have been ideal if Nobi had gone first. But somehow they had convinced Bodi to lead them. Now, it made the most sense for Nobi to take her turn. Then, if the other sisters (her included) didn't go through with the duke dare, at least the underlying objective had been accomplished.

Joan had her own objectives she was more concerned with, like the clandestine business she wanted to grow.

"Even though you're looking to increase the numbers of commissions you get, you'll have to spend a little less time hammering out daggers and a little more time hammering down a plan to snag a duke. It was the dare we all agreed to," Mimi said. And Joan couldn't help but notice a trace of smugness about the little one.

"And why don't you go next, Mimi?" Joan asked.

"I'm too young," Mimi said, crossing her arms.

"And a few weeks will make a difference?" Joan couldn't help challenging her. It could be the one question that might buy her some time.

"We can only hope a few weeks would make a difference," Bodi murmured.

"I heard that." Mimi stuck out her tongue.

"You were meant to."

"It makes sense that you go next for the duke dare, Joan." Coming from Nobi, Joan really didn't want to challenge her.

Yes. That. The dratted duke dare.

"Do you have anyone in mind?" Nobi asked hopefully. And Joan could read the room. The body language. Bodi: The expecting eyes. Nobi: The questioning eyes. Mimi: The challenging eyes.

Each sister was different, though they all got along. Each sister had their own unique talents and dreams. Bodi was well on her way. She was now about to start her girls' academy for fencing. The gossip was still floating around, but Bodi had the support of at least four dukes (one being her soon-to-be husband) that no one wanted to cross. More than that though, she had found love. And Joan was pretty sure Bodi had been the most skeptical of the four of them. Nobi was already in love. And Mimi was in love with being in love. And Joan…well, she was open. Just not as focused as Nobi. Or as driven as Mimi. Or as headstrong as Bodi.

"Well, do you?" Nobi asked again.

Right. The question. "No one in particular."

"What about one of Wes's friends? One of the Betting Buddies?"

Mimi raised her hand and smiled. "Chris is taken."

Joan chuckled. "Well, there were four." She held up her fingers. "Wes is taken." One finger went down. "Chris is taken." The second finger went down. "Samuel is far too competitive for me." The third finger went down. "So that leaves James. The—"

"—Duke of Cornwell. He's so handsome," Mimi interjected. "Thick dark hair, laughing eyes."

Yes, Mimi would say that. She was the first to point out the…manliness…of a man.

"He's—" Joan tried again.

"—so tall." Mimi's eyes were dreamy.

"He's a notorious—" Surely the third attempt would work in expressing her argument as to why she couldn't seriously pursue James.

"—jokester. And yet he looks strong enough to sweep me off my feet." Joan had to admit that the man could likely sweep any woman off her feet with a simple wink. He was dangerous, but knowing the danger was half the battle.

"Are we talking about me here or you, Mimi? Do you want to go after James?"

Mimi snapped out of whatever daze she had been in. "He's not for me."

"Really? Why not?"

Matter of factly, she said with a stony look, "He's a rake. I thought you knew that already."

"Yes. Well…" Exactly. There was no way that Joan, the quiet, calm, committed, and casually overlooked sister would have any interest in the reckless, daredevil of a womanizer who didn't want to settle down. Ever. No interest whatsoever. Not an inkling's worth. None.

— ❧ ❧ —

CHAPTER TWO

"Courage is not the absence of fear, but the triumph over it."
—Joan of Arc

THE WIND WHIPPING through James's hair. The thundering hooves banging down on the open field. The strength of the horse underneath him.

This was what made James feel alive. The rush. The recklessness.

He was racing his friends. That is, if one could call the insurmountable lead he had on the three, a race. At this point, they had no chance. They knew it when he suggested a horse race. But as usual, they agreed to it anyway. James would be the clear winner, and Samuel and Wes would compete for second, which they considered first place since James always won and therefore didn't count. Chris brought up the rear several strides behind.

Whenever James rode, which was frequent, he rode fast and hard. He couldn't be caught dead on anything less than the fastest stallion.

James stole a quick glance over his shoulder. The race would be over in three...two...one. He slowed Indra with a gentle nudge and a slight gesture on the reins. He might ride hard and fast, but he was nothing if not subtle in how he led a horse.

"I won," Wes shouted, while James had to hold back from jumping on that claim. It was futile to attempt to convince these two of his win.

"You did not," Samuel protested. And he would have sounded petulant with that rejoinder if he hadn't muttered it in a condescending tone. He raked his hair back with both hands, not even giving Wes a sideways glance.

"I was miles ahead of you, Sam."

By this time, Chris had caught up to them with a nonchalant look on his face. The man was the least competitive of them all, but he still indulged in a good bet. And even some bad ones.

"Right. So that spit from your horse's mouth didn't land on my gloves then?" Sam taunted.

"Exactly. I was ahead of you. You just admitted it." Wes did not look like he was giving up.

"Sure, Duke. You can take the win. Sounds like you need it," Sam said, as he shuffled the reins, collecting them in one hand.

"I don't need a win. I'm getting married tomorrow. That's enough of a win to last a lifetime."

Sam and James both belted out a laugh, Sam nudging James with his knuckles. "When did he become such a romantic nuisance?"

"All too soon," James said. "He's breaking up the Betting Buddies."

"Marriage won't affect us at all."

"It already has, Wes," Sam said.

Wes scoffed in a not-so-clearly scoffing way. It was more of a cough. And a laugh. With a bit of a humming sound.

"Might I direct your attention to the fencing tournament?" Sam lifted a brow.

"What of it?" Wes challenged, though all four knew he hadn't a leg to stand on.

"When you let your wife oppose me?"

"She wasn't my wife."

"Semantics, Wes. Really. You let the gel infiltrate our sacred, manly tournament." Sam was in full taunting mode now. James could see the flicker of amusement and mischief in his eyes.

"Don't call her that," Wes's voice rumbled over the empty field.

"Now, now," Sam said, knowing when to appease the beast. "We let her win the tournament—"

Wes's growl caused Sam to reword his statement. "We let her *keep* the win. But really, I hope you don't plan on inviting her to piquet tonight."

James snorted a laugh and tried to cover it up when Wes glowered at him.

"He's right though," James said, pointing at Sam. "I'd rather not see any women tonight while we're playing cards."

"Women or ladies?" Chris, usually the quiet one, inserted.

"Either," James laughed. "Or both."

"Really?" All three turned to look at him, likely questioning his sanity. Or perhaps his decision-making abilities. "Feeling quiet the rake today?"

James ignored Sam's comment, and turned to Wes. "We did the race, which was my pick obviously. We did the archery earlier, Sam's choice. Isn't it about time we head over to the club for Chris's pick?"

Sam was shaking his head. "I still think it's a bit odd that Wes is letting us three bacon-brains choose the activities of his last day as a single man."

"I don't need to do anything more. I'm ready to be married," Wes announced with an annoyingly bright, and immeasurably wide grin.

The other three groaned. At least, James thought the three were in sync. But really, he couldn't be sure about Chris.

"Let's go before this fool spouts any more nonsensical senti-ments on love and marriage," Sam said. He was already tugging on the reins to lead his horse to the club.

"Here, here," James agreed.

"Right then," Chis mumbled, following behind them.

Sam pointed up to a hedge in the distance. "James—"

Before he could finish suggesting the bet that James knew was coming, James took off toward it.

The hooves stampeded against the grass, beating out the

rhythm of James's heart. The hedge looked just above five feet high. It was high, but really, not that high. Not too high that he wouldn't risk the jump.

Blood pounded through his limbs. He blinked to focus and clear the glassy gloss coating his eyes. A bead of sweat dripped down the back of his neck. The moment was upon him. He could choose to direct Indra around the hedge, meet up with his three friends, and arrive at the club together.

Or.

Or he could risk it. He could jump the ruddy obstacle in his way, triumph over it, and beat his friends to the club by a minute or two. Worth it.

Not that beating them to the club was a factor in his decision. Really, the only factor was, could he do it? The answer was, probably. That was good enough.

He pressed into Indra, Hindu god of lightning and thunder, drawing nearer to his mane, and leapt.

JAMES SAT IN White's already nursing a whiskey neat by the time the other three strolled in. Chris was shaking his head the moment he caught James's eye. Sam had a goofy grin on his face, and Wes had a questioning eyebrow. Singular. Just the one, as if to say, *Really, James. Did you need to put your life at risk the day before my wedding?*

And if Wes had asked the question aloud, James would have answered in the affirmative. As it was, he just gave a smirk and a nod.

"Welcome. Took you all long enough," James said, lifting his glass in greeting.

"Yes, well not all of us feel compelled to engage in life-threatening activities at every turn." That was said by Wes in another condescending tone. Similar to what James would imagine an older brother might sound like.

"Good jump, James." Sam slapped him on his back applauding his achievements.

"Was that really seven feet high?" Chris asked.

James chuckled. "I could say it was, but I'd be lying. It was closer to five." He shrugged off the praise because he didn't take those actions in order to receive adulation. "I've done it before."

"Yes. Well," Chris shook his head, "looked pretty high from where I was."

"Aren't you glad you didn't take the leap then?" James asked. And of course the question was meant to refer to the hedge. And the horse. And the recklessness. But something in Chris's eyes conveyed that his interpretation of the question went much deeper than jumping horses.

"Yes. I suppose I am…" His voice trailed off.

Sam started slapping everyone on the back, telling them to sit and order drinks. He was attempting to harness whatever energy Chris was about to drain from them.

"Piquet, right?" Sam plowed forward.

"Before we eat?" Chris looked up from whatever rabbit hole his mind had fallen down, and all James could think was that someone could probably write a book about the journey his mind had just traversed.

"I'm famished. Food before cards," Wes stated.

So the four ordered food and quickly shoveled it into their mouths as fast as only healthy, male adults who had just finished a competition of sorts could do.

After the last few bites were taken, they each relaxed back in their chairs while Chris shuffled a deck of cards. Even after the meal, as short as it had been, Chris's mind hadn't entirely pulled free from the rabbit hole.

"You shouldn't have jumped, James."

"Stuff!" James stated a bit more harshly, a bit more defensively than he ought.

But Chris wasn't letting up. Ever the quiet one, he was choosing this battle to fight. "It's Wes's wedding tomorrow. Something could have happened."

"Nothing happened." James wanted to scoff. He wanted to shrug it off. It shouldn't be an issue. He was fine. But Chris was deceptively tenacious.

"Something could have."

"It's not my wedding," James argued.

"It could have been."

"It's not. And it'll never be." There. That ought to shut them up. Except, no. That was entirely the wrong thing to say. In hindsight, James should have had the wherewithal to *not* mock weddings, love, or marriage in front of the lovesick fool of a duke in their quartet. At the very least, he should have known that this particular group of men, on this particular day, at this particular time would not relinquish the small rope he had tossed them. Especially a rope tethered in marriage.

"What do you mean?" Wes's question seemed innocuous enough. It wasn't.

"I mean what I said. I'm not planning to get married."

Sam jumped in, "Well, no men really *plan* to get married, do they? Someone else plans it for them. A father or a mother sits them down one day and says, *Listen son, you're a duke. You need to marry and have a son. It's all for the dukedom, you see? We're all dukes. We've all had that talk, no?"* He didn't wait for any replies, just continued on, "And then when they do find the lucky betrothed—no offense Wes—the man doesn't *plan* the wedding. The future mother-in-law—or some female variety related to the betrothed—*plans* the wedding. Isn't that right?"

"Spoken as if you have firsthand experience," Wes eyed Sam.

"None. All second- and thirdhand." Sam smirked while Chris nodded along. Whether the nodding was in agreement or to keep the peace, James wasn't sure.

"All the same, I don't think that's what our dear friend James is referring to." Wes sent him a shocking look as he sat up in his seat. "You won't marry? You're the Duke of Cornwell. It's your duty."

"I think we all know how I feel about duty." He dismissed duty with a flick of his wrist. "It'll fall to my cousin. He'll do a good enough job."

"Good enough?" Wes almost popped out of his seat as those two words echoed in the room.

"Why are you so concerned? It's not your dukedom. It's not your life, Wes. It's my life. And I'll choose to live it how I see fit."

"Now, now. James doesn't want to marry and have children. Probably because his parents treated him like dirt. He doesn't want to perpetuate the cycle. Am I right?" Sam spoke the words cavalierly, as if they didn't shoot daggers into James's heart. Almost as if he were speaking about someone else. Not one of his best friends who was in the room, seated next to him, in fact.

It would be reckless for James to stand up and throw a fist in his face. But it would be impulsive. James was anything but impulsive. He took calculated risks, as uncalculated as it might look to any observers. So, although it would have been easy enough, and damn well satisfying to punch the sodding fool in the face, he sat in his chair with his hand around his glass instead.

"You're right," he said. And he almost left it at that, but then he had to add, "You sodding fatwit."

"Right. Well, now that that's settled. I have a question of my own. If you were to marry—yes, yes, yes, I know, you won't— but if you were to marry, what would have to be so special about the lady to make you fall for her, assuming you'll only marry for love?"

As if that were a given…it wasn't. James wasn't planning to marry. He didn't want to marry. There was no bone in his body made to love. Or be loved. He had always known that. Always would.

"Not going to happen—"

"Indulge me, James."

So James thought of the most ludicrous checklist of requirements he could think of off the top of his head. But of course, he tapped his chin lightly before he spouted off the list, as if to relay to his friends that he had given this any amount of thought prior to Sam's question.

"Well, there are three things, if I had to put them into words and onto a list." Tap. Tap. Tap.

"Which you do."

"Thanks, Sam." He tapped his chin a few more times. "First of all, she has to be willing to name her first daughter December."

"James—" Wes started.

"Let the man speak," Sam said with terse lips. Was he suppressing a smile?

"Secondly, she has to have a mole in the shape of a moon on her backside."

And then, just because he was on a roll and he could see Sam struggling to keep himself in check, he added, "Thirdly, she must kiss my eyeball."

"Oh my God, James, give it up." Wes slapped the table. "Let's play piquet before this chucklehead starts drinking."

There. That was the response James was looking for. Get them off his back. For now.

CHAPTER THREE

*"Believe in yourself and all that you are. Know that there is
something inside you that is greater than any obstacle."*
—Joan of Arc

BOUDICCA LOOKED BEAUTIFUL as she walked down the aisle. Full of strength. Full of life. Love. And hope. Joan had never seen her sister look more fully herself than when she walked forward into her destiny. It was a destiny that Joan had never thought possible, and she knew Bodi felt the same way. Did that knowledge give Joan hope? It should. It meant that love existed. Love was all around, if only a person were open to it.

It was marriage, but it was also so much more. Boudicca's academy for girls was now part of her future. These were things that Boudicca had desired for so long, and now they were finally coming to fruition. All because she took a chance on love. Maybe more so because love first took multiple chances on her…but all the same. Love was giving Boudicca everything she had ever wanted. Joan was so happy for her sister and m aybe just a touch jealous. Not that she wanted Wes for herself in any way, but just…well, really…a future with someone you love and who loves you sounded rather nice.

The ceremony was taking place in Bellator Manor in the Practice Hall, with Boudicca walking down the aisle toward Wes. Although the Practice Hall was hardly recognizable with all the adornments and flowers.

Seeing her sister carry her rapier alongside the bouquet made Joan smile.

But the moment that Boudicca handed that rapier to Wes…Joan couldn't stop the tears. It seemed such a foolish thing to cry over. But it was the gesture and the sentiment behind it. Boudicca wanted a partner in life. Someone who could challenge her, but also someone that could appreciate her strengths. Particularly when that strength overshadowed his own.

It was a rare man indeed who could appreciate a woman having an edge over him. And rarer still to find one that would celebrate that strength.

So often women had to hide their talents, their wisdom, their intellect. All because of the fragility of the male ego. If any one of the sisters had remained a spinster, Joan would have predicted Boudicca. She would never settle for anything less than perfect. Needless to say, Wes was perfect for her. He would be her partner in every way. Sharing the rapier was almost a gesture of equality in the partnership. Each of them had their strengths, and they celebrated that fact.

Being a witness to this great love was bittersweet. Joan couldn't help thinking how profound yet how uncommon such relationships were. It was exceptional, in every definition of the word. Leaving Joan feeling anything but exceptional. She was confident in who she was, but she also knew that she was often under the shadow of blonde beauties like Bodi and Mimi. Whose attention might she catch? She couldn't imagine.

To think of whom Joan might pursue as part of the duke dare they had all agreed to, made her stomach flip over. It might have even rolled out a few somersaults for the amount of queasiness she was experiencing.

But she shoved those thoughts and feelings down for now. For as long as she could. Well, at least for the ceremony. This was supposed to be a sacred moment.

And it was. The vows that were shared between the two brought a fresh wave of tears to the sisters, and by the end of the ceremony, their handkerchiefs were saturated. Thankfully, the reception would not provoke any teary responses. The dinner and toasts were done, and a dance was underway.

Taking a short break, Joan stood with her sisters Mimi and Nobi watching the dancers.

"I can't believe she's married," Nobi said in awe.

"If I hadn't witnessed the ceremony I might not believe it myself." Joan eyed the couples twirling about on the floor.

"I knew it would happen." Mimi gave them a sideways smirk.

"Is that so?" Joan asked.

"It's always the most resistant who fall first."

"You,"—Joan placed a heavy emphasis on this first word in case Mimi wasn't paying attention and then for good measure repeated the word—"you think Boudicca is the most resistant of us four?"

Joan watched from the corner of her eye as Nobi stifled a chuckle.

Without hesitation, Mimi retorted, "Of course she is. Who do you think it is?"

When Joan caught Mimi's eye, both she and Nobi announced at the same time, "You."

Mimi just waved her hand in dismissal, as if that small flick of the wrist could disabuse them of such a long-held notion. And really, it wasn't just that it was long held, it was rightly held. Artemisia was the hellion of the four. Case in point, one: she was the one who suggested the dare. Case in point, two: she never held back vocalizing her opinion. Case in point, three: her opinions were often in opposition to those around her. Case in point, now: her being resistant to the idea that she is the most resistant.

"You don't see yourself as being resistant?" Nobi asked gently.

"No."

"Not even say…right now?"

"Pfft…this is not me being resistant. Not really. At least not the kind of resistant I'm talking about. I'm open to love. I'd argue that I'm the most open to love out of all of us."

Well, really, Joan didn't have a rebuttal for that one. Boudicca had been a closed door, inside of a vault, under a rock. Nobi was like a timid child afraid to ask for what they wanted. And Joan…she wasn't sure how to describe her heart's openness to love. She supposed…she was open…enough. But perhaps she needed to know more about this openness that Mimi spoke of.

"How are you open to love?" Joan humbled herself to ask her little sister for advice.

"I'm so glad you asked, Joan." Mimi's eyes twinkled. "Everywhere I look I see the opportunity for love. The possibility for love, marriage, a future…it's all around us. Any one of these gentlemen could be yours."

Joan could almost hear the words as if they were coming from a hawker on the street. Someone selling a tincture that could heal gout, relieve a fever, erase all a person's debts, and make one fall in love.

If one simply bought it. And drank it.

Her skepticism must have been showing.

"You may laugh at me. On the inside. But I can assure you. Gentlemen are just as willing to fall in love as women are. They just don't know it. And if perchance they do, they will definitely not admit it. There's nothing so debasing to a man as sharing his feelings, especially pertaining to love."

"What about poetry and all the men who write it?" Joan challenged, just to amuse herself.

"Pseudonyms." Mimi didn't even blink, which caused Joan and Nobi to chuckle behind their fans. "It's really written by women."

Mimi swept her arm out to showcase the dancers, "Now tell me what you see."

"Dancing," the two said together.

Mimi rolled her eyes. "Let me tell you what I see. I see love taking aim. A man approaches a woman. Curious. Obliged. Or otherwise. And love is watching. Waiting. She'll take aim and if she has a good shot, she'll let her arrow fly."

"Ah, I see where this is coming from now," Joan sighed. "You are the archer. Perhaps you relate to cupid more than I would have predicted."

"Perhaps," Mimi volunteered noncommittally as her eyes surveyed the room. "Look over there. See those two men."

"Don't point, Mimi," Nobi said.

"Just follow the line of my fan. Better yet, look for James. See who he's standing with?" When Joan nodded with Nobi, Mimi continued, "That's Lord Jacob Fenway." The two nodded again waiting for further explanation on Mimi's tangent.

"He's pining over our dear friend, Lady Sally Prohope. But, as we all know, Jacob is too shy to approach Sally on his own. Ahh…what tragedy, that two people so close to love might not find it. See how Jacob has enlisted James to help him? At least he has that much sense. Now the question is…who will go help Sally say yes to love?"

"How do you know Sally wants to find love?" Joan regretted the question immediately after she asked it. Surely Mimi would whip around and a long rant on *love for everyone* would ensue. Surprisingly, Mimi maintained her vigilant scanning of the ballroom. When she spoke, it was calm, albeit a touch patronizing.

"There are two universal truths to humankind. We all want to be loved. We all want to belong. Mark my words, Sally is looking for love. And if neither of you are willing to help her, then I'll—"

"No, no, no. I'll go help her." Joan volunteered before Mimi could finish her threat. Because really, it was a threat. If Mimi, in all her assertiveness (one might call it), went over to assist the soft, timid, fragile Sally, who knows what kind of love she might find herself in?

Mimi practically pushed Joan in her direction. "Go on then."

"You do realize you're the youngest, don't you?"

"Argh, such is my cross to bear. But bear it, I shall. Now go."

"I'm going," Joan insisted.

"Good luck," Nobi whispered in parting.

"Pfft…luck. She won't need any luck." But Joan didn't stand around and ask what Mimi meant by that. She took a few brisk strides and found herself at Sally's side.

When Joan stopped, she almost said, *Sally, I'm so glad you could make this event. It's been too long since I've seen you.* But then the conversation she just had with her sisters floated through her mind. If Sally wanted to be loved and was actively looking for love, perhaps she could attempt a more coy greeting. They were close friends after all.

So instead of the casual bland greeting she would usually use, she asked, "Do you see him watching you?"

Sally started.

And for a split second Joan thought she asked the most addle-pated question of her existence. But then…as Joan watched Sally's face, she saw a timid half smile tempt her lips. And if that weren't enough of a giveaway, her cheeks flushed. When Sally brought her fan to her face and fluttered it a couple of times, Joan knew that she had hit her target.

And when Sally uttered a breathless, "Yes," well, then Joan knew a few more things. Sally noticed Jacob watching her. Sally enjoyed that fact. Jacob, with enough courage from James (the rake!) would approach and ask for a dance. And Joan would be there to support Sally in saying yes. It was all so simple.

Joan's heart almost clapped in joy. Love could be a beautiful, simple thing. It could just be one (or two, if one insisted on counting James) person helping a friend find courage to love.

Love didn't have to be complicated. It didn't have to be en-twined, wrapped up, coated in layers, and tied with a dare. Daring a duke had nothing to do with love for Sally and Jacob. Shy Sally. Always with a softly spoken word. A gentle soul. Pure and innocent. She was in love with the boy who was too shy to ask. But once he did ask, Joan knew that the floodgates of love would open. Or perhaps, to stick with the metaphor from Mimi, love would take aim and shoot her arrow (yes, cupid is female here because, well...Mimi).

It was simple. Innocent. This moment of helping her friend was already opening Joan's eyes to love. Perhaps her heart would follow.

CHAPTER FOUR

"There is no agony like bearing an untold story inside you."
—*Joan of Arc*

A S SHE STOOD there, with her opening, Joan realized that this was the perfect opportunity to learn more. The more she knew, the better she could help. If all it came down to were each person taking courage, speaking to each other, and saying yes to love, then Joan already knew the plan. If there were any complications that should come to light, it was better to know them up front rather than later on down the road.

"What have you noticed?" Joan asked because she was in it now. She may as well dig deep and find out what she could. So she stood at Sally's side as the two of them observed Jacob and James a few yards away. The two gentlemen were having a tense discussion, despite the tight smiles on their lips. Joan was pretty sure that James was trying to convince Jacob to do something. If not to invite Sally for a dance, at least to converse with her. And now that Joan was with her, there wouldn't be as much pressure. Four people made conversation easier than two shy people.

She sighed in thought, and finally answered Joan's question from behind her fan. "His dark hair."

Dark hair. That was a good reason to be smitten. If one was into dark hair, Joan supposed it was attractive. Though really, it ought to be as dark as James's hair if not darker for one to really see the appeal.

"Ahhh...and his blue eyes." All right. That was more information, although of a similar depth level to the first point. Dark hair. Blue eyes.

True. Jacob's eyes were a nice blue. If one liked the pale-robin's-egg color over looking into the ocean of James's eyes when one spoke.

"So...is that why you..." She didn't know how to ask Sally if she loved him. That felt too direct. "You feel the way you do about him?"

"I'm in love with him." At that announcement Sally closed her eyes and exhaled softly. "I can't help it. It's overtaken me. I'm afraid I'll do something reckless with him."

This was headed in the right direction. In fact, this was exactly what Mimi had observed. Jacob was pining. And it looked as though Sally was pining the same way. "So if he asks you to dance, you'll say yes?"

"God, yes. I've been waiting. I'm almost of a mind to walk up to him myself and ask him."

This was news. Good and bad news. Bad only if Sally acted as recklessly as she suggested. It was not done for a woman to ask a man to dance. But the news was also good. Good in that perhaps Sally didn't need her help at all. It seemed that this was a fairly one-sided deficiency. That of Jacob's. All he needed to do was ask, and Sally was all his. Joan could feel her heart rejoicing again. She needed to take action to help Jacob take action, so that Sally didn't take action and make a fool of herself. Or worse, cause a scandal. Sweet, shy, innocent Sally. The last thing she needed (the last thing any woman needed) was a scandal.

Joan looked up, trying to catch James's eye. It was a bit awkward, since the two of them hadn't really conversed before. But...well, oddly, it was simpler than she thought it would be. When she looked up, he was already waiting. So once she caught his eye, she took a half step back to be out of Sally's peripheral vision. Then she tilted her chin toward Jacob. James pointed discreetly to his friend with his hand on his chin and Joan nodded.

Then she canted her head toward Sally and James nodded.

Wow. For never really having a conversation with him, that went smoothly. She would have never thought that communicating with a stranger, a male one at that, could be so…effortless.

And then she saw James give Jacob a soft tug on his arm. Say something to him. Which she could only hypothesize was something manly like, *Get your wits about you. Ask the chit to dance.* When Jacob shook his head slightly, James made another comment and Jacob's eyes went wide. Slowly he nodded, and James patted him on the back. Hard. Likely with a twofold purpose. One, to congratulate him on making the right decision. Two, to give the man some forward momentum and take the first step forward.

It was all going according to plan. It was all so simple. Joan couldn't be more delighted.

"He's coming," Sally squeaked.

"Yes, he is. Are you ready?"

"I can't believe it," she said, her fan fluttering faster than Joan had ever seen a woman flutter a fan before. Another whisper-squeal, "It's happening. It's finally happening. My mother won't like this one bit, but I'm so happy."

And that last sentence gave Joan cause for concern. Why would her mother not be happy? Jacob was perfectly respectable, albeit a bit shy. There was no reason—

"How do I look?" Sally was breathless. To the point that Joan thought she might be a likely candidate to swoon.

"You look beautiful. Take a deep breath. You don't want to swoon before he has a chance to ask you to dance."

"No, you're right." She panted. Panted! Despite standing still with her shoulders nearly at her ears in tension. "Wait. Maybe if I swoon he'll catch me in his strong arms and then he'll carry me away."

"All right, Sally." The plan was not so simple right now. Sally needed to calm down or everything would hit her fan and scatter everywhere. The fan was still flapping at a preposterously rapid pace. "Let's think this through. We have two seconds before he's here. You can have a first dance in his arms, fully present with him, or you can fall in his arms semi-conscious. Which is it going to be?"

And really, Joan thought she had laid out that question as if there were only one preferred option. Yet Sally paused before answering.

"The dance," she decided, as if it were an epiphany. "I'll go with the dance. Oh, thank you Joan. Thank you for being here. I don't know what I would have done without you."

At this point, Joan wasn't sure what she would have done either.

And just as the two men approached, Joan caught James's eyes again. His ocean-deep eyes. He raised both his eyebrows in greeting, giving her ample space to plunge into his depths. Her breath caught.

"Lady Joan." More depth rumbled out of him, this time in the form of his voice, as he made the introductions.

And Joan almost forgot the concern that had been a flag in her mind from a moment earlier. Except she couldn't forget the concern because all of a sudden James was flicking his eyes at Sally. And then back to her. And then at Sally. And then back to Joan.

Joan was confused.

James cleared his throat.

Joan was still confused.

James canted his head toward Sally. And raised his eyebrows again.

Finally Joan looked over at her friend.

And…

Oh.

My.

God.

The flag of concern was raised. It was blowing in the wind. It was quite the largest flag she had ever seen. And it was crimson red.

Jacob was staring at Sally. Besotted. Predicted. Expected. Going according to plan.

Joan was staring at Sally. Questioning. Dumbfounded. Because while James was staring at Joan, also questioning, Sally was staring at *James*. Dreamily.

This was all wrong.

This was all so wrong that Joan didn't think it could be worse.

Wait. It was getting worse. Sally was slowly raising her hand toward James.

This was what Joan had feared but not enough, and not toward the right man. Joan had thought it would cause scandal if Sally were to ask Jacob to dance. A respectable gentleman. But oh—Joan cringed—it was going to be so much worse if Sally asked a notorious rake to dance.

So Joan did the only thing she could think of. The only action that made sense in the moment. The only action that could save her friend from scandal, and more importantly, inevitable heartbreak later. James was a rake. He would never settle down, especially not for shy, quiet women like Sally and Joan. She wasn't quite sure why she included herself there, but that wasn't the point. The point was that she needed to act quickly. Before Sally could embarrass herself, Jacob, and James.

Joan threw a fake smile on her face and extended her hand toward James, "I believe this dance belongs to you." She didn't want to outright lie in front of the group, but she would deal with her conscience and this misleading white lie later.

It took James less than a second to reply. In fact, no one could have guessed that she had just sprung this on him.

"I do believe it does," he said, taking her hand. And he turned to his friend, "Don't you have something to ask Sally?"

Jacob beamed at Sally, thankfully oblivious, "May I have the honor of this dance with you?"

Joan was shocked that Jacob had managed so many words. Given his earlier state, she would have thought his words would have been a jumbled mess.

But no, it was Sally's words that were the jumbled mess.

"Oh, erm…the dance? Well—"

Joan looked at her friend and mouthed the word, *yes*. She tried again with, *say yes*, but still no reply.

"What she means is yes," Joan answered for Sally as her friend gave her a bewildered, and perhaps a little disappointed look.

"Yes, thank you," Sally finally said, but the dejection was solid in her tone. Joan felt compelled to act quickly again. She couldn't go forward in the dance knowing she was hurting Sally. Rather, with Sally feeling hurt. They were different. Really, because Joan knew that in the long run she wasn't hurting Sally. She was protecting her.

"One moment, James. Jacob, if I may." She took Sally's hands in her and rushed a whisper. "You can't show James how you feel. He's a rake. If he sees you wearing your heart on your sleeve, he'll eat you alive. Be calm. Pay attention to Jacob. That kind of behavior might make James jealous."

"You are so right, Joan. So wise." It was a boon how trusting Sally was. And it completely reinforced Joan's resolve to protect her from James. With how trusting Sally was, it was inevitable that she would find herself out on a terrace with a rake. And then a scandal. Fortunately Joan was around and Sally was willingly putting her trust in her dear friend.

Joan could see that Sally's eyes seemed to clear from whatever fog had descended upon them when Joan had announced her dance with James. In fact, Sally almost looked relieved, if Joan was putting a label on it. Her shoulders were no longer at her ears. Her voice was back to a normal pitch. And more importantly, her fan had ceased fanning.

And even though Joan half-hated herself for deceiving her friend, she could not—would not—let her friend fall for a rake. This was the only way to save Sally's heart. Surely if she spent enough time with Jacob she would fall in love with him. Joan was praying to the love gods watching this all unfold. Praying that love would take aim—more accurately this time. And then once it had its opening…

Shoot.

Chapter Five

"I am not a book."
—*Joan of Arc*

J AMES WAS LEADING Joan onto the dance floor when she tugged on his arm before the music could start.

"Is there a problem?" James asked over his shoulder.

Oh yes. There was a problem. Joan was not about to dance with a rake, if she could help it. Being led to the floor by him looked bad enough. She hadn't actually planned to go through with the dancing part.

"We're not dancing together."

He laughed. "Not yet, but—"

"No. Not yet or later or anytime. I need a refreshment. I'm feeling—"

With a waggle of his brows, James jumped in— "mischievous?"

Joan just rolled her eyes. "Let's just get a drink."

"You don't have to ask me twice," he said, leading her away from the dancers. Thankfully they still had time before the instruments reverberated with sound. Still holding her hand on his forearm, Joan and James found a spot where they could stand discreetly together. It was as if he had read her mind in placing them here.

Here. Where they were apart from the crowd enough to discuss the goings on of the evening. Here. Where they could watch their respective friends hopefully find love. Here. Where (hopefully) no one would judge Joan for spending some time in the notorious rake's presence.

Taking a sip of his drink, James watched as Jacob shone a brilliant smile at Sally. And Sally…well, she reflected a blurry version back at him.

"So," James didn't look at her as he spoke, "are you going to tell me what your plan is? Or shall we continue to test our nonverbal communication skills?"

He noticed it too, then, did he? That was an interesting observation to make…if she were making observations about James. Which she wasn't.

"I can't dance with you." Joan decided to take the direct approach.

"So I gathered by the fact that we're not dancing." The amusement in his voice was vexing. Was he laughing at her? Didn't he realize the risks she was already taking?

"You're a—erhm…well, you know"—the direct approach was not always so easy to take—"you must know…that you're a rake,"

James's hand flew to his chest, his mouth falling open. "I can't believe you said that." His aghast whisper shouldn't have given her lips a reason to smirk.

Blasted mouth!

"James, don't be silly. We have only a few minutes to scheme."

"Scheme? I like the sound of that. If I weren't holding a drink, I would rub my hands together and cackle," he said this with a sideways glance and a wink.

"You can still cackle."

"I'll save you the embarrassment of the eyes you don't want on you. I understand you're ashamed of me." He shrugged nonchalantly, but something in his tone made Joan pause.

"I'm not ashamed of you."

"Don't worry yourself over it. You wouldn't be the first. And

I'm sure you won't be the last." After a large gulp from his drink, James rested his glass on a passing tray and picked up another.

And even though he had reassured her that she shouldn't care about how she felt, she felt she needed to reassure him that that wasn't how she felt. Or something like that.

"James," she said his name gently, and when his ocean blue eyes met hers, she spoke more sincerely than she intended. "I'm not ashamed of you. I'm sure you are a good man. But I'm a lady, and I have a reputation to maintain. So does Sally. That's why I couldn't let her dance with you."

"Well, we agree on one thing. Sally can't dance with me. Jacob will be heartbroken. He's smitten."

Agreement. That's what Joan liked to hear. "Perfect. We are in agreement then. We must show Sally that falling for Jacob is in her best interest. Or, at the very least, that falling for you is in her worst interest."

"Ouch!" James's hand gripped the fabric around his chest. "You wound me."

"I doubt it. I'm sure you've heard worse."

"True. So true," he mumbled. James scanned the room and switched his drink to his other hand. He took a step back and leaned against a pillar to further obscure him from view. "What's the plan? Shall we stage a rescue? Plot a scandal?"

"Why would we stage a rescue?"

"Don't all women dream of being rescued by a strong, handsome man?"

Joan, in all her elegance, harrumphed at that. "I think not."

"You've never dreamed of swooning and falling into the arms of a man you found attractive?"

Well, she wasn't saying *that*…and sure, Sally had just expressed something eerily similar, but really…to think that all women did was wait around to be rescued…well, that was just…silly.

"Let's discuss Sally, shall we?"

James laughed at her reply, counting it as a win of sorts. And really, it was.

"Sally needs some…encouragement. Jacob is a gentleman and a worthy eligible bachelor. If we can just shift her attention to him enough, I'm sure she'll fall for him."

"Yes. Proximity is the number one reason a couple falls in love in the first place."

"It is?"

"Well, you can't very well fall in love with a man you've never met or spoken to, can you?"

"I suppose not…though I'm sure somewhere some woman has."

"Some woman somewhere is not most women everywhere. Let's scheme according to the most likely rather than the exception, shall we?"

"Agreed." Joan sipped her lemonade in thought. "Perhaps he can call on her tomorrow with flowers."

"That's average at best."

"It's the safe, predictable approach."

"And where does safety get you?" he asked mockingly.

"It's got me this far."

James stared openly. In fact, he took that moment to stare at almost every inch of her. Down to her slippered feet, which he couldn't see but she felt as though he could, and all the way up to the crown of her head. His perusal unnerved her.

"What are you looking at?"

"You."

"Yes, but what are you looking for?"

"Your suitor."

"You beast!" She almost swatted him, but held back. And then decided to swat him anyway. "I have had suitors." A few. None that she had any interest in. None that had been of particular interest to anyone. And if she was being truthful, none that showed a unique interest in her.

"All I'm saying is that you've played it safe, and you have no suitors."

Joan crossed her arms in defiance and her eyes began a steady crawl up and down his body. Trying not to notice how his thighs filled out his breeches. Or how his arms strained at the seams of his jacket. Or his broad shoulders. None of those things mattered. Especially not the slight bulge she caught sight of accidentally, causing her to blush. No. She was trying to make a point. If he could study her, then she could study him.

"What are *you* looking at?" She knew he would ask that, so she played her hand.

"You," she said simply.

"And what are you looking for?"

"Your wife."

He barked out a laugh. "Well played, Joan." He chuckled again and wiped the mirth from his lips with a giant palm. Oooh! His hands were large. And smooth. "The difference is, I don't want a wife."

"That's quite arrogant, isn't it?"

"What?"

"You're saying that you don't have a wife because you don't want one. But you're implying that you could have a wife the second you did want one."

"Look at me, Joan."

"I have."

He chuckled. "I'm a duke. I'm handsome. I'm wealthy. Young. And respected enough. I guarantee you that if I wanted a wife I could have one from this very event, despite the small crowd."

And she knew he was right. There was absolutely no point in arguing with him. No point. Whatever point she would make would be, well, pointless. She made it anyway.

"You might be able to find a wife, but that doesn't mean you'd have love."

He scoffed, and it irked her. "I don't want that either."

"You don't want a wife?" He shook his head. "You don't want love?" Another shake. "What about the dukedom?"

"That shall go to my cousin."

"That's just irresponsible."

"Really? I think it's rather the most responsible thing for me to do given my mother—"

But she didn't let him explain.

"You're reckless. You throw caution to the wind and don't care if anything bad happens."

His eyes darkened. "You're overly cautious and you're too worried about even the possibility of something bad happening."

"You think everything is a joke."

"You take everything too seriously."

At this point, Joan was baffled and disoriented. How had she thought that there was any connection between them? The ability to successfully communicate across a room was pure luck. They were two completely different people. She wanted to put more space between them. "Your cologne is too strong."

"I can hardly detect the lavender scent you're using to entice the male population."

"You probably spend your days drinking and gambling."

"And riding." He smirked. "And you probably spend your days reading."

He wasn't wrong. Again. The man was a nuisance.

"You obviously harbor resentment toward your mother, and my Mama always said that you could tell the character of a man by how he treats his mother."

James's ocean-blue eyes turned stormy, "Only a controlling and self-serving woman would say that."

"I'd ask you not to speak ill of the dead." Joan had stepped right in front of James, only a half of a foot between them. She was infuriated now.

But then James closed his mouth. She expected another retort. When he still said nothing, she supposed even a rake knew when to keep his mouth shut.

"I'm sorry," he murmured. But it wasn't the words that spoke to her. It was his hand. His fingers had somehow found hers and were sweeping side to side over her knuckles. It was wildly inappropriate, but she couldn't pull away. It was a tender gesture. Even his eyes had calmed.

"It's fine."

"It's not—"

"Let's just discuss Sally and Jacob."

"Fine." And Joan wasn't sure if he said the word in jest or not.

Joan took command of the conversation. "When the dance is done, we should greet them and explain how I needed a drink." James nodded along, obviously placating her now. "And then we can suggest that Jacob pay her a call tomorrow. Perhaps go for a carriage ride."

"Wait. What if she tries to wrangle me into a dance again?"

"She won't." The arrogance of this man. To think that Sally would act so contrary to societal norms and ask him for a dance. Again.

"But what if she does?"

"She won't." Joan said with vehemence. Really, the man needed to be knocked down a few pegs.

"How can you be so sure?"

"She just danced with a man completely besotted with her. Surely she felt something. I can't see her being audacious enough to try again. Especially in front of Jacob." Joan knew Sally. She was quiet. Shy. Of course she would fall for Jacob, she just needed to be placed in his arms for a dance.

"But she might…"

"She won't."

But then she did.

Chapter Six

"Do not be afraid to stand up for what you believe in, even if you stand alone."
—Joan of Arc

WELL, THIS WAS about to get ridiculous. Joan watched as the supposed-to-be-in-love couple approached, and she could see the coy look in Sally's eye. Directed exclusively at James. Joan wanted to groan. And roll her eyes. And stamp her foot. And maybe just cart Sally away from the rake altogether. But of course that was not possible.

She thought her pre-dance advice had been sage and accepted. Apparently not.

"I could use a refreshment after that dance," Sally said demurely. It was almost comical how she dipped her chin, fluttered her lashes, and peeked up at James while she said it. Joan challenged herself to keep her groans to herself.

Jacob didn't notice a thing, the poor besotted fool. "I'll go grab us some drinks."

"Thank you, Jacob," Sally said while eyeing James. Once Jacob was out of earshot, Sally did not relent. "Oh, is that another dance?"

Why yes, that is another dance. During a ball. That tends to happen.

"Are we all lacking a partner?" Sally asked without concern for her reputation or her future.

"Actually," James started and paused. And Joan knew that he was giving her time to step in and decline the offer that she knew he was going to make. How she could read this man so quickly and easily already was terrifying. "Since Joan is hydrated now, we will have this dance together."

And there it was. The exact response she had been formulating in her mind. Despite their differences, it was apparent that James shared one invaluable trait with Joan. Loyalty. James wanted Jacob to win the girl, so he wasn't about to get in the way of that. And Joan was loyal to Sally's reputation, and despite her friend's lapse in judgment, she wasn't about to let her make a foolish mistake.

One might think that Joan was about to make a foolish mistake by dancing with the rake she was trying to protect Sally from. They would be wrong. There was one clear difference between Joan and Sally. Joan wasn't halfway in love with James. And she never would be.

It was one dance. Yes, there may be a little bit of gossip, but nothing that Joan couldn't diffuse. It was an intimate ball, her brother-in-law was a duke, and she was simply dancing with one of her brother-in-law's best friends.

So, with that reassurance…validation…justification…excuse…Joan said, "Yes, that was what we decided." And she took James's hand making their way to the floor, leaving Sally all alone. Well, now that wasn't true. She was soon to be in Jacob's ever-loving care.

"Don't say it," Joan preempted James's *I told you so* before he could produce the four disdainful words.

He chuckled. "Well, I did say—"

"You're saying it."

"It can't be helped. It's rare when a man gets to prove a woman wrong, isn't it?" His smirk was just enough teasing, just enough affection, just enough arrogance to be just a little irksome. But somehow it was doing things to her heart as well. Things like melting it.

Serendipitously, James took that moment to twirl her, giving her a chance to catch her breath and collect her liquifying insides.

When she spun back to face him, she decided to concede his point. "Well, if you're going to say it that way, I suppose I can accept to hear it."

"Wonderful,"—he paused, exhaled to savor the moment, and then blurted out—"I told you so."

A small chuckle escaped her lips unbidden. "I know when to admit my mistakes. I was wrong. I'm rather shocked to admit it, though I'm more startled to witness it—since I've known Sally for ages. But my friend is not as predictable as I once thought."

"Is anyone?"

"I don't mind saying that I'm quite predictable." Besides her secret pastime and hidden token, she was quite predictable. It was not a trial to confess that.

"Are you?"

"Yes. I think I should know myself."

"Would you have predicted that you would be dancing with me tonight?"

Her steps faltered. Damn this man. She really did not want him to be right twice in her presence, and so close together.

Silence was probably the best approach. That is, until he chuckled. And pressed his hand more firmly into her back. A nudge, if there ever was one. A nudge to encourage her to admit yet another mistake. A nudge that brought her an inch or two closer to him. A nudge that she wanted to ignore but couldn't.

"Fine." She huffed. "You are right. Again. I'm the cautious one. Predictable—usually—and I'm always watching out for the people around me."

"If you're busy doing that, then who's watching out for you?"

An excellent question. Really, one that she should be asking herself. "Boudicca." She sighed. "Any of my sisters, but more often than not it has been Boudicca." She let her eyes scan the room for her newly wedded sister. She was nowhere to be seen for this dance. Likely she had snuck away with Wes for...a moment alone. Joan didn't permit her mind to consider the intimacies between the two of them. Especially not right now while she was in the arms of a handsome rake. She was allowed to say that. His physical achievements were undeniable.

"She's married now. That changes things." James interrupted her thoughts.

"Yes, that's very perceptive of you."

"I'm a very perceptive man."

"So I've perceived."

His light chuckle rumbled through his fingers. The warm, strong fingers holding her and leading her through a waltz. And she couldn't help but appreciate how good it felt to make a man laugh. Any man? Or this man? She wasn't sure about the answer to that question. But at the very least, it was a light, frilly, feathery feeling to be able to make this man laugh.

"What are we going to do about our friends?" he asked and then swung her away from him, only to bring her back a second later. Truly, he was an elegant dancer.

"Should we do anything?" She didn't really mean it, but she wanted to ask the question anyway.

"They're made for each other. She just doesn't know it yet." How intriguing that James should think so too. Was it that obvious to everyone? Or only those closest to either Jacob or Sally? Or was James as perceptive as he claimed to be?

She wanted to know his answer. "Is that so?"

"You don't think so?"

In fact, she did think so, but did she want to agree with a rake?

"Well…" She found Sally on the sidelines sipping a lemonade. Surprisingly, she wasn't watching them dance. Instead, she was talking with Jacob. A small smile lit her face. "She's in love with you."

"No, that's not love." He said it so matter-of-factly that Joan was compelled to challenge him.

"She thinks it is. How can you be so sure it isn't?"

"First of all, love doesn't exist. Second of all—"

"Wait. That was a rather large first of all. It warrants some discussion."

"Not sure it does." James hummed as though he was pondering her prying statement.

"Trust me." She paused to consider her next move.

"I do."

That flustered her. "You do, what?"

"I do trust you."

"You do?" Well, that was odd. He hardly knew her.

But he didn't expand upon it other than to say, "You seem trustworthy. I'm a good judge of character." Then he winked and added, "Trust me."

And…she wasn't sure if she did or not, so she let that jest go unanswered.

"About love…" She still wasn't sure what she wanted to say at this point. Try to prove its existence? Seemed an unlikely achievable goal with the time constriction of a single dance. Maybe a simple challenge? Or just a statement of her opinion on the matter?

"Yes. What about it?" His eyes were glimmering. Almost hopeful. Eager for her response. She had better make it good.

"Yes, well, love is love." That should do it.

He threw back his head and laughed. "I couldn't have said it better myself."

Flustered, Joan pushed the conversation along. "What's your second point as to why Sally couldn't love you?"

"Ah yes…Second of all, even if love did exist—which it doesn't—she doesn't know me."

"Perhaps she knows enough."

"She thinks she knows enough," he corrected.

"You don't believe in love at first sight then?"

He looked down at her then, and she wished he hadn't. His ocean-blue depths almost pulled her down and away from having her feet on solid ground. She blinked to dissolve the moment, but he continued gazing into her eyes. She had to wonder what the devil he was looking for.

"I would say no, I do not believe in love at first sight." But his response did not sound as confident as nearly everything else the man said. "It doesn't matter what I believe about love." Joan watched his corded neck swallow, knowing there was more to this than what he was disclosing, but she could see he wasn't willing or ready to discuss it.

He plodded on with his point. "What signifies here is that Sally is better off with Jacob. We both agree on that, don't we?"

"Yes, that's true." She really couldn't not agree with that. Especially since anyone would concede the point.

"If she thinks she's in love with, or even if she is in love with me—which I highly doubt—then we need to redirect her attention to Jacob. If she sees who I really am, and sees who Jacob really is, there's no question whom she'll pick. For marriage," he added the last two words with a wink.

Joan skirted her eyes away while the blush crept up her neck.

"How do we do that? How do we get them to fall in love?"

"There are a few tactics we need to implement." His eyes glimmered in mischief. Joan could appreciate that the duke liked to scheme. "First of all, of course I'll avoid her as much as I can. If that means I end up at your side a little more frequently than before, so be it."

A flutter swept through Joan's body. "Why would you be around me more?"

"It's a safe bet." Another wink. "Also, if she thinks I'm interested in you at all, that might deter her affections."

It seemed sound. But Joan's mind was fully fuzzy at the moment, and sound wasn't sounding as it should. Her mind (which at the moment was overtaken by her body) was focused far too much on the warmth of his hand on her back as his thumb slowly brushed up and down about an inch worth of space. That inch of space on her body had never felt so alive.

"Second of all, whenever the four of us are together, I'll be sure to pair up with you. And you'll do the same."

She nodded along, though she wasn't entirely sure what she was nodding to.

"And the last part, the falling in love, is the hard part. Wouldn't you agree?"

Her eyes were glued to his lips. Soft-looking lips. Lips that had kissed many women, and from the rumors, kissed them well. What would it be like to be kissed by him? His lips were moving. He was saying words. And she was pretty sure he was waiting for her to say something.

"Wouldn't you agree?" she heard the question now, but what it was in reference to, she wasn't sure.

"Would I?"

"I thought you would." He gave her a quizzical look.

"Then I'm sure I would." That seemed the safe answer.

"Splendid. We'll discuss this further, but this will have to do for now." He leaned in and whispered something that if she had been paying attention didn't need to be communicated, "The dance is over." And then he was removing his hand from her back. And she was pulling herself back together from the liquid puddle she had become.

What had just happened? One minute Joan had been perfectly in control of herself, her thoughts, her body, and the next second it felt as though all those parts of her no longer belonged to herself. Her thoughts had vacated her body, perhaps even the ballroom. Her body moved at the whim of a thumb tip. A thumb tip!

It must just be the wedding. And talk of love. The environment was setting a mood she hadn't expected to succumb to. And really, what kind of man spoke of love and marriage to a woman? It was unheard of. That's why marriages were arranged. Didn't James know anything of how polite society worked? No matter, now that Joan understood why she had been so affected by their dance, she wouldn't allow for it to happen again. Really, there wouldn't be the same opportunity again anyway. It's not like they would find themselves dancing together again at someone's wedding talking about love for a second time.

$$— \; \oe\,\mathcal{O}\,\mathcal{O}\,\mathcal{O}\,\mathcal{O}\,\mathcal{O}\,\mathcal{O}\,\mathcal{O}\,\infty \; —$$

CHAPTER SEVEN

"Do not repeat the tactics which have gained you one victory,
but let your methods be regulated by the infinite variety
of circumstances."
—*Sun Tzu*

Two Days Later

JOAN FOUND HERSELF at another wedding. A house party wedding. And here she stood in the ballroom that was decorated with more flowers than the eye could take in, not really looking for James. But if her eyes happened to catch sight of him, she wouldn't be upset.

Mimi was making comments about the floral decisions. Something about the white lilies meaning pure love alongside the hyacinths being charming. Or was it the other way around? She wasn't sure. And as she caught sight of a tall dark-headed man in the corner she tried to avert her eyes. But her heart was hammering in her chest. Why it should be doing that, she wasn't sure. But if James was here, she just wanted to be prepared. That's all.

"Joan?" Mimi's impatient voice rang through her thoughts, her fingertips tapping against her crossed upper arm. "Are you even listening to me?"

"Of course. Liles. Love. Hyacinths. Charming." It should satisfy Mimi that she could regurgitate a few words back.

"We've moved on from the flowers, Joan. What are you woolgathering about? A daring escape with a highwayman at midnight?" Mimi was always so dramatic. "Being rescued by a pirate on the seven seas?"

"Where do you come up with these ideas, Mimi?" Nobi asked, while placing her hand in her dress pocket.

Mimi tapped her temple, implying the power of her over-worked imagination. "And books, of course," she said with a twinkle in her eye. Mimi was perhaps the most voracious reader of all the sisters. Any genre, but mostly romance (as was made obvious by her sharing her fantasies), was her preference.

Joan was relieved that the focus had shifted from her to her sister though. She really didn't want to tell her sisters anything about James. Because…well, she wasn't really sure what there was to say. Unfortunately for her, the relief was short lived.

"Are you going to tell us, Joan? Or do we have to drag it out of you? What's on your mind?"

Dragging usually didn't sound pleasant, but if they pulled bits and pieces out of her, that might help her process what she was actually thinking. And she wanted to talk to her sisters about James—even though she didn't—so she asked the next best thing.

"Have you seen Sally tonight?"

"Yes, I saw her earlier. So you're not going to tell us about your dance with James the other night?"

"No." Joan answered dismissively. "Where did you see her?"

"Fine." Mimi released her crossed arms. "We should seek Sally out then and find out what's going on with Jacob," Mimi said it as if it were a suggestion, but the sisters knew it was as good as a command.

"If we all go, that might be a bit overwhelming. We don't want to bombard the poor girl. I'll go find out what's happening, and then I'll report back to you."

Mimi gave her a dubious look, and then must have decided that that course of action seemed logical. "Fine," she agreed.

Joan started walking in the crowded ballroom. She kept re-turning one hand to her right pocket for more reason than just habit. But it did help to avoid being bumped, even marginally. With the people around her, she was itching for activity other than a society event though. She didn't mind the balls, actually enjoyed dancing (enough), but she preferred a more invigorating pastime. She would get to it when she had time. She could already envision the target.

For now, Joan's search for Sally was on though.

Which was good. Because if she found Sally, she would probably find Jacob sooner rather than later. And if she found Jacob, well, James might be there, too. If he was, he was. And if he weren't, that was fine too. It was a tad distracting that she should keep thinking of his large frame and his firm, but graceful movements on the dance floor. That dance. She sighed. It had been…nice.

She shook her head, refocusing on her mission. Sally and Jacob. Specifically, Sally.

Ah…There she is.

Joan grabbed a couple of drinks from a passing tray as she walked over to her friend. Handing one to Sally, she greeted her with a smile.

"You're so lucky," Sally sighed.

Joan tried to hide her surprise. "Oh? Why do you say that?"

"You've been spending so much time with him." Him. Joan knew who *him* was. He was the *him* she was not hoping to see tonight. Just open to the idea of seeing him.

"I wouldn't say so much time." It was only a lemonade and a waltz.

"You danced with him, did you not?" Sally's eyes had turned dreamy, and Joan had an inkling that the scheming to get Sally and Jacob together may need to be taken up a level, but how?

"I did dance with him."

"Was it more than you could have ever imagined?"

Well, it was certainly more than Joan had ever imagined. But that was because she had never imagined it before. However, since that dance, she had imagined it again. On occasion. And she had been prone to wonder if a second round of dancing would surpass all the imagining she had done since not imagining him.

"It was…nice," she said flatly, giving voice to her own assessment of the event and hoping to deter Sally from asking more questions.

Her glassy-eyed friend only exhaled again. "Oh, to be held in the arms of a man desired by so many."

Joan did not want to dissect that statement, so she asked about a (hopefully) safer topic. "Did Jacob pay you a visit after your dance?" It was only normal for a gentleman to pay a call or send flowers to the ladies he danced with. Joan was hanging onto hope that Jacob's gentlemanly honor trumped his timidity.

The question seemed to shake Sally from her dream state. "Yes, he did." A smile—true, a very small one, but it was a slightly curled lip all the same—formed on her face.

"That's lovely. Did he bring you flowers?"

"Of course, he did." Sally eyed Joan directly, as if to say she had just asked a ridiculous question.

"Not all men bring flowers, you know?"

"Don't they?" Sally was paying attention now. She turned her body away from the dancers to fully face Joan.

"The Duke of Baskim didn't bring Boudicca flowers on his first visit." And Joan regretted letting that juicy tidbit slip from her lips the second she heard the masked glee in Sally's reply.

"You don't say?"

Joan cleared her throat. "He—" She had no idea how she was going to finish that sentence. Doing her best to make it sound like Wes wasn't a complete nincompoop. "He forgot." Yes, that was her best in the moment because it also happened to be the exact moment her eyes caught sight of a dark-headed waltzing wonder. Not that she thought that of James. But some women somewhere did.

"I can't believe the duke forgot flowers."

"He made it up to her, don't worry." Joan rushed the words in an attempt to shush Sally so that she could concentrate on James's movements. And then she realized that it was utterly foolish to track the dratted rake. She had far better things to do.

Like, pretending she wasn't following his every move with her eyes.

And even though she wanted to retract her clipped tone and replace it with the full story, she realized that Sally hadn't even noticed because all she responded with was a hissed, "He's here." As if Joan needed the reminder.

James caught her eye, half-smirked, and walked in the opposite direction of her and Sally. Joan exhaled, not realizing she had been holding her breath. Of course, James wouldn't approach. He didn't want to encourage Sally in any way. But what had the coy look been about?

"How do I look, Joan?"

"You look beautiful as always, Sally. But you needn't worry. He's not coming this way," she said, turning to Sally more fully and ignoring James's presence.

"You're probably right. Perhaps we can try to make him jealous again? Do you really think that plan would work?"

"It's human nature to want what you don't have."

"I don't have him yet, but that doesn't mean I can't have him," Sally rejoined.

Joan held back on replying to that. Sometimes what a person didn't have was for good reason. Like in this case. James was a notorious rake. A womanizer. He used women to bed. How many more ways did she need to say it? James was not looking for marriage. Did Sally not care that her reputation was on the line? That even if she did snare James, he would likely end up resentful of her and her scheming ways? That was no way to live a life: the object of someone's resentment.

But Sally wanted what she didn't have. What she shouldn't have. And, in spite of her shyness, she was insistent in asking, "Wouldn't you agree?"

Joan shrugged just as a man approached her side. She was about to be inwardly grateful for the distraction when she recognized the male figure. Lord Tamely extended his hand saying, "May I have this dance?"

It was rude—disgraceful even—to decline the man, despite him being a weasel. So she took his hand and was swept across the dance floor. But it wasn't a nice, gentle sweeping, like how a woman might feel light on her feet, dancing on air even. No, it was a sweeping sensation as if she were a broom, being handled.

"Are you enjoying your evening?" the weasel asked.

"Yes," Joan chose a monosyllabic response in an attempt to discourage further questions.

"It's a nice night for a wedding, isn't it?"

"Yes." She added a half nod with this reply so as not to appear too impolite. And she worked up a half smile to add to the half nod to round out the two halves and make a whole. Though inwardly she wholeheartedly cringed.

Thankfully the dance was short, and Lord Tamely was leading her back to Sally. It couldn't have been more perfect timing because just as she was walking up, so were Jacob and James. She could feel James's eyes on her, piercing the skin on her hand where Lord Tamely was freeing her from his forearm.

If Lord Tamely could have read the room, or at least the small group he was in, he would have quickly acknowledged that he was the fifth wheel. Unfortunately, he had no such abilities of perception.

"Tamely, didn't you say you were going to dance with Lady Simone this evening?" James gave a curt tilt of his head which Tamely didn't misinterpret.

"Quite," he said, bowing and taking his leave. Though he gave one last look at Joan, and then at James. Turning to Joan, he said, "It was lovely dancing with you." And he kissed the air above her hand.

And just before Joan could worry about Sally making another move on the wrong man, James stepped up. Again. "I believe this dance is mine."

Another dance. Another dance with the rake. Surely it wasn't so bad to agree to it. After all, it was saving her friend, who she could see from the corner of her eye taking Jacob's hand to the dance floor. They both had a slight blush, and Joan could only hope that they would see (and quickly!) how they were made for each other.

James didn't waste any time in getting to the heart of the matter. "Is love blossoming?"

Startled, Joan drew her eyes up to meet the ocean tide she knew awaited her. "What do you mean?" Could he read her? She didn't even know what was going on inside of herself. Her heart was hammering. Here she was. Dancing with the rake. Again. At a wedding. Talking about love. That's all the fluttering was about. The same damn environment had been recreated. Joan took a slow inhale to calm her nerves. And whatever that mad fluttering was in her stomach.

"Those two." He canted his head in the direction of Sally and Jacob. "Are they in love yet?"

"I don't think it happens that quickly." Though…she couldn't really be sure.

"We need to do more. Did she say anything to you about Jacob?"

"Not really. Just that he brought her flowers when he visited."

James blew a raspberry with his lips. "Every man does that."

"Not every man…"

But he didn't answer her with more than a curious brow. "Every man should. It's a moot point. He did it. He should have done it. Now he needs to do more. Are you sure she didn't say anything else?"

"She just mentioned you."

"What did she say about me?" he asked with a waggle of his brows, possibly searching for one of the many compliments he knew was passed around the gossip circles.

"Just that you're…."

He winked at her and spun her around. "You can tell me."

"She said she wanted to be held in the arms of a man desired by so many."

"That's good." James looked impressed, and even a bit enlightened. "We can use that. She's not really interested in me, just the idea of me. We need to give her a better idea of Jacob."

"But Jacob is nothing like you."

"Exactly. But maybe she just needs a new idea about Jacob. How quickly can you convince your sisters to start spreading a few bad rumors about a good man?"

CHAPTER EIGHT

*"Treat your men as you would your own beloved sons. And they
will follow you into the deepest valley."*
—*Sun Tzu*

WITH THE LAST notes echoing in the ballroom, Joan left
James's arms to find her sisters while James made his
escape to a card room. After a minute of searching, she found her
sisters each taking a bit of a lemon square. Thankfully they
weren't dancing. She needed to have this conversation with them
immediately. If they could implement this plan, then Sally and
Jacob had a chance of becoming a couple.

"Mimi, Nobi, I need your help," Joan whispered over the rim
of her lemonade. "Well, Sally needs our help."

Mimi's troublemaker eyes glimmered in the excessive candle-
light. "What do we need to do?"

"Is Sally in trouble?" Nobi, ever the peacekeeper, asked.

"Sally is fine. But Jacob is in love with her. And Sally…is—
erm…she thinks she's in love with James."

"Your James?" It wasn't an innocent question that Mimi
asked. Joan knew she was fishing for information; she could see it
in the twinkle of Mimi's eyes. Also, this was her youngest sister.
She rarely, if ever, had a simple innocent agenda.

Joan blushed. "He's not my James."

"You've danced with him twice this week," Nobi added. And
Joan had to admit that Nobi was probably guilelessly bringing

that up.

"Those are just dances. It's not like someone caught us alone on the balcony together." Joan huffed. "They were just *dances*," she repeated in her strong defense. Dances in his strong arms, with a warm hand on her back. Protective. Guiding. Enticing. No. Not enticing. Just existing. "They were nothing."

Mockingly, Mimi raised her fist in the air dramatically and hissed, "Nothing I tell you." She laughed. "Methinks the lady doth protest too much." Then she capped her performance with a wiggle of her brows.

"Mimi, please. This is not about me. This is about Sally. We need to protect her reputation. She's far too forward with James. She's basically asked the man to dance three times this week." Joan exhaled. "It's been exhausting trying to keep her away from him."

Mimi and Nobi exchanged glances while Joan picked up a lemon square of her own. Her sisters were obviously communicating something, she may as well grab a treat. "Are these any good?" But she didn't wait for either of them to nod in approval before taking her first bite.

Sublime.

Just what she needed right now. Since her sisters still weren't saying anything, Joan picked up the conversation again. "Sally is much better off with Jacob. We all agreed."

"We did?" Nobi asked.

"We did," Mimi confirmed, with a nudge to Nobi's ribs.

"James and I discussed it after we three did. Sally and Jacob make the perfect couple. If only Sally could see it." She didn't think she needed to remind her sisters of their conversation, but their lack of words prompted her to fill in some gaps.

"Yes, I completely agree," Mimi affirmed, nodding her head.

Wait. That was strange behavior from Mimi. She was *completely agreeing*? Unlikely. Nobi was normally the agreeable one. "What do you mean, Mimi?"

"Just what I said. I agree. Sometimes a person can't see their perfect match when they're right in front of them. And they just need a little…nudge." Mimi poked Joan in the arm.

"Stop that." Joan swatted at Mimi's index finger coming in for round two. "Sally thinks she's in love with James—"

"And she's not?" Nobi asked.

"Of course not. The man's a rake. She just thinks she's in love with him because women everywhere are swooning over his obsidian locks and ocean-colored eyes. And his broad shoulders aren't deterring her either."

Nobi and Mimi's eyebrows shot to the ceiling. "Yes…well, those features could fell any woman," Nobi drawled.

"Perhaps," Joan dismissed the idea. "Many a woman might fall for James, but not me. I can withstand his charm because I know the truth about him."

"Which is…?" Mimi left the question hanging in the air.

"He doesn't want a wife. And he never will."

"Is that all?"

Joan narrowed her eyes at Mimi. "Is that all?" she repeated the question. "That's enough for any gently bred lady. The man doesn't want a wife. There's no point in falling for him."

"I'm not sure it works that way," Nobi said cautiously. It was as if she were trying to say something without really saying it.

"What way?" Joan asked, needing more details.

"You don't exactly choose who you fall for." Nobi's explanation did little to appease Joan.

"Of course you do." Joan expelled a puff of air. "You choose to love someone, and then you still have to choose to love them every day."

"That's a different kind of love," Nobi clarified. "I'm talking about who you fall for. You don't get to choose that. Sometimes you just"—Nobi sighed raggedly—"see his eyes and…fall. Hypothetically, that is."

"Anyway, that's not the point," Joan plowed on not wanting to delay the plan to gossip about Jacob. She knew how Nobi felt about Chris. It wasn't the kind of love she ever expected herself to feel. It was too rare. And she was too ordinary.

"Isn't it? Aren't we trying to make Sally fall for Jacob?" Mimi asked.

"Yes. And it's simple. If we can just spread some rumors of Jacob's…prowess…and erm—desirability—then Sally will see that other women want him. She'll be jealous and fall for him."

The sudden silence between the sisters was exasperating. Did she really need to spell it out in more detail for them? Did she need to break down the phonetics? Surely they could see how the plan would work. But they were just looking at each other, communicating using their eyebrows and a side pout of the lips.

"What are you two discussing?"

"Nothing," they said together.

"So will you help me?" And then she added, "And Sally?"

"Of course we will."

And it only took four dances, six more lemon squares (split evenly between the three), and a few drips of *on dit* spilled over the rims of three glasses of lemonade to get the rumors started.

I hope Jacob asks me to dance.

I hear Jacob knows how to please a woman.

I'd like to meet Jacob in the gardens.

Have you noticed the size of his hands?

Jacob? The man with the swoon-inducing eyes?

And from there the rumors escalated. So when Joan found herself watching Sally from a few paces away, she was delighted to see Sally watching Jacob as he asked another lady to dance. It wasn't a fiery jealousy that Joan detected in Sally's eyes, but the slightest curiosity. Which was much more than what she'd seen before.

"The plan is working. Meet me on the balcony in five minutes." The deep voice rumbled over her ears, just loud enough for her to hear. And just low enough to resonate in her bones. Shivers ran up the backs of her arms. There must be a breeze in the room.

From the corner of her eye, she watched as James popped out

onto the balcony using the furthest door at the end of the room. She needed to update him on their progress, so she may as well do it now. Taking a quick stroll around the room, she made her way to the same door she had seen him exit.

When she stepped out into the fresh chilly air, an extended hand greeted her with a drink.

"Cheers to us." James's voice sent a warm jolt to the pit of her stomach.

"You saw how she was looking at Jacob?" Joan's giddiness was evident in the tone of her question.

He nodded in the darkness, only half of his face lit by the moonlight. She could still detect a small smirk.

Taking a sip of her drink, she pulled back in surprise. "Champagne?" It was uncommon for ladies to drink champagne. Lemonade was their expected drink of choice. Especially since the fiasco that was the night of the duke dare, Joan had been extra cautious of what she was drinking. All four of them were already heavily immersed in a dare that would affect their entire futures. She didn't need another feat to her list of impossible things to accomplish. Securing one duke was enough.

"We're celebrating," he said with a wink. Lifting his hand, he waited for her to mirror his gesture, then he clinked the glasses. "To us. And to love."

Of course, he was referring to Sally and Jacob's blossoming love, so the swelling warmth she felt in her belly meant nothing. Must be the champagne.

Joan took that moment to appreciate another sip of her drink and then looked up into the night sky. The stars above twinkled with minimal cloud coverage. It was a still, serene night, with only a slight chill in the air.

"Are you cold?" he asked softly.

At the same time, the chill of the air sent goosebumps up her arms.

"No, it's a nice night."

"Here. Take this." He was already divesting himself of his

jacket and swirling it around her shoulders before she could protest. His heavy cologne enveloped her in a spicy, masculine scent. With as much discretion as she could muster, she inhaled deeply, letting the scent fill her nostrils. It was an odd thing to consider committing a scent to memory, but she pondered it anyway.

If they hadn't openly discussed their differences, and if she didn't know of his plans never to marry, she might think of him sharing his coat as a meaningful gesture of sorts.

She mumbled a quick, "Thank you." Then she leaned back against the balustrade. It was best to focus on business, not jacket sharing and heat-triggering scents. "What's our next move?"

"Tomorrow Jacob wants to take Sally out on the pond to go rowing. We'll go with them." James was close to her, his hip pressed into the same balustrade she was leaning against. He was within arm's reach. She could easily touch him. His chest. His bicep. His forearm. Not that she was thinking of that.

"You stated that as if it's already decided. As if I don't have a say in it."

He peered at her over his glass, taking a small sip. "Would you prefer we didn't go with them?"

She shrugged, unsure of why she was resisting the plan. "It seems like a good enough plan. No possibility of scandal."

He laughed. "Right. We must avoid scandal at all costs."

"You say that in a mocking tone?"

"I do."

"Why?"

He gestured to the balcony. "We're alone on a balcony."

And then it hit her. She was alone on a balcony with a known rake. What was she thinking? She had only been thinking to update him on their progress and possibly make further plans. When had she let her guard down?

Seeing her panic, he chuckled again. "It's fine. We're done here anyway. You can return inside. Safe. Unharmed. Untouched." The last word he lingered on. And she couldn't help wondering what more touches from him might feel like. But that path led to ruin.

"Yes. That's a good idea." Not the touching. The returning inside. "Here's your jacket." She took her free hand to slip out of it, but it was falling too quickly. It was on its way to the ground when James reached behind her and caught the jacket. In the movements, his arm latched around her waist, and she was pressed up against his chest.

His solid, warm chest. With each breath she felt its friction against her breasts, and her nipples were responding.

Her breath hitched in her throat. "Thank you," she said hoarsely, not really sure why she was thanking him for saving his jacket from hitting the ground.

His voice was just as hoarse. "You're welcome." His eyes studied her face. Dropped to her lips. He licked his bottom lip and then dragged his eyes back up to hers.

Joan's heart hammered in her chest and she was sure he could not only hear it, but feel it as well, thumping against his chest.

"Joan—"

"I thought I saw her go outside." A new voice entered the conversation from just beyond the door. Joan couldn't quite distinguish it from the roaring in her ears.

Suddenly her back was pressed against the exterior wall of the building, her front was crushed against James's back as he stood hiding her from the incoming scandal. His body, in conjunction with the opened door was enough to camouflage her in the darkness. She felt…protected.

"Is she out here?" That voice was definitely Mimi's, and Joan sighed in relief.

"I don't think so—Oh, James. I didn't see you there," Nobi said.

"Just getting some fresh air." James's voice was shockingly calm.

Joan tapped James on the back with her index finger to com-municate. When he moved to the side, she stepped out from behind him.

"Oh!" Nobi startled.

Mimi's face split into a grin, but all she said was, "There you are. We were looking for you."

"We came out to discuss our progress on Sally. The rumors seem to have aroused her curiosity." *Aroused?* That was the wrong word to use. Too late.

"Splendid," Mimi said with a clap of her hands. "Everything is going according to plan."

CHAPTER NINE

*"The supreme art of war is to subdue the enemy
without fighting."*
—*Sun Tzu*

JAMES WAS FEELING off. At first he attributed the feelings to the fact that he hadn't lain with a woman in a while. But if he were being honest with himself, he had only noticed that he had been feeling a little bit off since Boudicca's wedding. More specifically, since his dance with Joan. Or perhaps just before that even. The conversation over lemonade had already prickled his…what? His heart? No, surely not. His nether regions? Yes. That was true. Something in his body reacted to Joan, that was undeniable. But he was a rake, and he had plenty of reactions to countless women.

Except…

The way he responded to Joan's smile. Her laugh. The slight touch of her hand. Those were different. He could honestly say he had never had such strong physical reactions to such innocent gestures. When he danced with her, she fit in his arms so perfectly. And when he had hidden her on the balcony, it was to protect her. Not out of self-preservation. Though he still didn't want to marry, his instinctual reaction had been to preserve her reputation. She was somehow charming, despite being so practical. And her brand of charm particularly charmed him. But when he stopped to think about it, which he didn't do all that much, he chalked it up to the weddings and all the talk about love.

Really, they mostly spoke of love and marriage and helping their friends fall in love, so it couldn't be helped that new—and odd—feelings were teeming through him. James pushed those reflections aside.

Under bright sun and blue skies on this fine afternoon, his previously mentioned plans were about to come to fruition. The house party guests had been invited to a picnic, and everyone was lazily gathering in various groups on blankets or chairs provided. Jacob, however, was not of the lazing variety, and James could feel the nervous energy bouncing off of his friend.

James had suggested to Joan that there was no harm in priming Sally for the boating invitation. Since she had seated herself next to Sally, it was no hardship to do that.

"Wouldn't it be lovely to sit in a rowboat on a day like today? To feel the breeze on your face while out on the pond," James overheard Joan point out to Sally.

"That sounds quite nice," Sally said, flitting her eyes over to Jacob who was practically itching a hole into the selection of fabric that was covering his knees. "If only someone were interested in the activity."

Joan had told James that Sally was shy, but so far, every interaction James had observed of Sally was of her putting herself out there, so he couldn't help but wonder about Joan's people-reading skills.

Thankfully Sally wasn't focused solely on him anymore, she actually seemed to be a bit curious about Jacob. If that were true, this afternoon could trigger their courtship. Unfortunately, Jacob was too wrapped up in his nerves to notice Sally's invitation, so James nudged his friend.

"Don't you have something you want to ask?" he whispered to Jacob, raising his brows.

"Uh…oh…yes, erm—Sally," he cleared his throat, "would you like to accompany me on one of the rowboats?"

James jumped in as well so that the two weren't going off on their own.

"Joan, shall we join them?"

"Yes, that would be wonderful," she said, pushing herself to stand up.

Samuel and Chris had joined the picnic and were sitting with Joan's sisters. And just before the two couples departed, Samuel whispered into James's ear, "One hundred pounds Jacob gets too nervous and sinks his boat with Sally in it."

James bumped him with his shoulder. "God, I hope nothing so dramatic happens."

"Have fun!" Mimi shouted after them as she lounged on her blanket.

James took Joan's hand and placed it on his arm, leading her towards the boats.

Making conversation, he asked, "Do you know how to row?"

"I do. Do you?"

He chuckled, amused at how she could turn the simplest of phrases on him.

"Yes. Do you know how to swim?"

"I do. Are you planning something I should know about?"

"Nothing of the sort, just curious."

"Curious about anything else?"

Actually, he was quite curious about her. She could be cagey when she wanted to be. At other times he could see her open up to him. Even though he wasn't interested in her, and he knew she wasn't interested in him (due to his rake status), there were parts of him that wanted to know parts of her.

He stole a glance at her. She was rather beautiful. Dark hair, almost matching his. And deep-green eyes like a forest. The sharp slope of her nose. The soft curve of her kissable lips. Yes, he could admit to them being kissable. Any man with a pulse would concede the point. She was beautiful. Not for him, of course, because she was a lady. Which meant she was looking for marriage and children. The exact future he was avoiding. If he weren't avoiding that future, he would certainly be keen on exploring her body. He wanted to see her naked. That escalated. But once the thought was there, he wanted to see more of her. Her sprawled on his bed. Or skinny dipping in the pond at night. He really shouldn't entertain such thoughts. With his height, and from his peripheral vision, he could see her creamy mounds teasing him. He should be thinking that they were nothing he hadn't seen before. But he couldn't quite get there in his mind. They were something—

"You're staring at me," she interrupted his thoughts without looking at him. "You're either curious about something or I have something on my face."

"I'm curious," he confessed. And because he was feeling off, and he didn't want to be the only one suffering, he blurted out, "Have you ever gone skinny dipping?"

He expected her to whirl around and march off before they could even get their boat in the water. He half expected her to sock him in the arm for some reason.

Instead, all she said (without looking at him, mind you) was, "Wouldn't you like to know."

And yes, now he really would like to know. Before he had just asked to startle her. Throw her off her equilibrium. But that plan hadn't worked, so now he was verging on desperation to know the answer.

But he wasn't going to get that answer. At least not right now. They had arrived at the boats, both pulled ashore, and Sally and Jacob were getting in. Which meant that they were now within earshot. He had little doubt that Joan would give up any revealing information in their presence.

James offered Joan a hand into the boat. "Steady now. I'll hop in and push off using the oars."

With grace, Joan alighted and sat balanced in the boat. James hopped in and with a giant push, set them off into the pond.

With a quick turn, James rowed, his back to the pond, staring at Joan. "Can you see them?"

"Hardly," she said, shifting her weight to look around him. "But what little I can see indicates that Sally might be switching her focus from you to Jacob. Not sure how much longer we'll be needed."

A pang stung James near his chest. He was enjoying this time around Joan. If he didn't have much time left with her, he wanted to know more about her.

"Tell me something no one knows about you."

Silently she eyed him, and he could feel her skepticism scanning him. "If no one knows it, why do you think I would tell you?"

"Sometimes it's easier to tell something to a stranger."

"While I wouldn't call you a stranger, I can see your point." She sat back in thought.

After rowing for a minute, just when he thought he would need to ask a different question, she spoke up.

"You know that Boudicca fences?"

"Yes."

"My thing is daggers."

James studied a small blush creeping up her neck, and he smiled. "What do you mean exactly? What do you do with daggers? Are you a clandestine knife fighter?"

"No. I throw them, and I'm a bladesmith."

Stunned, James stopped rowing. "Wait. You actually make the blades?"

"Mostly daggers. They're my specialty. I'm always carrying one."

"Like right now?"

She nodded.

"When we were dancing?"

She nodded again.

"When you sleep at night?"

"Not that it's any of your business what I do at night, but I do keep one close at hand."

"Wow. You are an impressive lady, Joan. For being so predictable, I'm shocked."

"Thank you."

When she said those two words, it was as if she wanted to say more, so he waited, hoping that she might trust him. For some unknown reason.

"Sometimes people commission blades from me." She looked up at him, and the light in her eyes actually stole his breath. She was the most excited he had ever seen her. "They don't know it's me. I hope to grow my business one day."

Her confession warmed him. She was trusting him with something incredibly important to her. And though he didn't know why she was doing it, he felt...appreciated. Maybe that wasn't quite the right word. He felt included, a sense of belonging, and strangely, it all felt right. It felt as though she should always confide her secrets in him.

"You won't tell anyone, will you?"

"Of course not. Your secret is safe with me." He remembered to row again. After a few strokes, they were now obscured from view by some large hedges and trees growing in a tall clump at one part of the pond. "I never knew you were such a daredevil."

"I'm not really—"

THWUMP.

"What was that?" Joan asked, putting her hands on either side of the boat, she stood up. Well, she half stood up. What she was really doing was bending over in half to look over his shoulder (he knew that was to be the real reason). But the tiniest part of him wondered if she was trying to show him the depths of the valley between her two jostling mounds.

He could feel his arousal twitch between his legs.

"Could you"—he cleared his throat—"sit down?"

She didn't budge. "What happened?" In fact, she leaned closer to him, giving him an even clearer view.

He groaned.

"We hit a rock, James."

The urgency in her voice caused him to glance behind him.

Sure enough, there was a boulder in the middle of the pond.

Irritated more by his body's reaction than their small boating accident, he cast the blame her way. "You didn't think to warn me that we were headed toward a boulder?"

"I didn't see it behind your mountainous frame."

She thought he was big?

"Your shoulders are too broad."

"Is that a bad thing?"

Flustered, she answered in a rush. "No. I mean, yes. I mean…erm…that's not the point. I just couldn't see around you." And then, probably because the air between them had grown thick, she added, "Or maybe it was your big head I couldn't see around."

He laughed, jarring the boat.

"Oh, James. Don't laugh," she scolded.

"Why not? It's funny."

"You're rocking the boat." And then she went down on her knees in front of him. Down on her knees! She was practically between his legs.

"What are you doing?"

"There's a small puncture in the boat." Her voice was panicked. "Water is seeping in." She looked around the empty boat. For what, he did not know. Hammer and nails? A bucket? "Quick. Give me your stocking."

"What?" he screeched. That was certainly a sound that he had never produced before.

"I need to plug the hole."

"Use your own stocking."

But really, that was the wrong thing to say. He knew that it was the wrong thing to say when he watched her lift the hem of her dress to reveal rim ankles, and—he couldn't look. He also couldn't let her continue.

"Never mind. I'll give you mine."

But he must not have been working fast enough, because as he unlaced one shoe, she was working on his other.

"Don't move, James. You're moving the boat too much."

But he had to move. He had to get his sock off. He had to do something to not think about her potentially between his legs, touching his foot. Skin to skin.

And then the potential disappeared and became reality. She *was* between his legs. Pressing up against his cock (now semi-hard), mumbling to him not to move (which he didn't dare do), and thrusting forward. Toward the hole he could only presume. With stocking in hand.

He squeezed his eyes shut. No one could see them, which at this precise moment was both a blessing and a curse. For this was a scandalous position to be found in. The curse however, was that if he didn't row them back fast enough, they might sink. And even if she could swim, her numerous layers would weigh her down. And though now more than ever he wanted to see her skinny dipping (for then he would have firsthand knowledge of the answer to his question from earlier), he didn't think that skinny dipping in front of so many guests would preserve her reputation.

"Hurry up, Joan."

"I'm almost…there. Yes."

"I don't need your commentary on it," he said, gripping the oars with power from the almighty above.

But she didn't quit. "So close." He squeezed his eyes shut and clenched his jaw.

"Just…need to…finish…yes. There!" she exclaimed.

God, that was torture. "Get up," he shouted.

"No need to growl at me. I'm trying to save us."

He glared at her and started rowing them back to shore.

"Oh dear, the stockings aren't working."

"What?"

"Can't you see the water collecting in the bottom of the boat?"

Yes, he could see it. Now that he was looking at it. But no, he hadn't seen it because he was trying to keep his eyes up and away from her or anything near her.

"The boat is going to sink before we get to shore," Joan stated the obvious.

"Hell," James muttered. This was a terrible situation. Should he jump in the water and take some weight out of the boat? The hole was just high enough that without his large frame it might bob above the waterline.

Well, better him than her in the water. He started to take off his outer layers.

"What are you doing?"

"Swimming."

"Now?"

"It's so you don't have to."

"Oh."

And then he stood up, ready to jump.

— ❦ —

CHAPTER TEN

"Ponder and deliberate before you make a move."
—*Sun Tzu*

"DON'T JUMP!" A clear, female voice rang out. It wasn't quite panicking. But it was a warning, yet laced in hope. James stood still, widening his stance so as to reduce the wobbling of the boat.

When James looked up, he saw Joan's wide eyes. "I think I see Jacob and Sally. Let's wave them down. You don't have to jump in the water if we can get their attention. They're just over there." She pointed at a beige-and-brown cluster poking out of the water.

If he didn't have to dive into the water to save them, he would much prefer that. James glanced behind him and there behind some cattails was the edge of Jacob's boat. Now that he was looking for it, he could see it. "They can't see us yet."

They waited, anticipating the boat would come into full view shortly. Nothing.

"Jacob!" he called out, realizing the boat wasn't moving. They waited again eagerly. Surely Jacob heard that. Nope. What the deuce were they doing? There was no reason to stop on the water and look at a forest of cattails. Unless…and well, James was a man. A virile man. He could think of a reason or two to pause, hidden from view.

Did he really want to disrupt *that* if it was happening? But his options were limited. One: Sit in a sinking boat. Two: Jump into a lake to save himself. Three: Interuppt a friend's prospects.

"Jacob!" James called louder.

Nothing.

James directed his attention to Joan. "Together, on three." When she nodded, he counted down. "One. Two. Three."

"Jacob!"

It was impossible for James to believe that Jacob didn't hear that shout. And then sure enough, the tip of the boat inched forward, and the rest of the boat came into view. James planned to discuss his observations with Joan later, but suffice to say, he noticed Sally tucking her hair behind her ears and smoothing it back into place. Her lips looked a little swollen, and her cheeks were tinted pink. And Jacob…well, he was bearing the widest grin he had ever seen on any man.

But any analysis of those observations would have to wait. And though he felt a small pang of guilt in how he hindered his friend, he more highly prioritized Joan's safety in this situation.

"Jacob, our boat has a hole in it. Come over here and take Joan to shore." Now that he saw the size of their boat and eyed the four bodies needing to fit, he wasn't sure they would all be able to clamor inside the one rowboat. So much for his options. Swim it would be.

"What about you?" Joan asked.

He quieted his voice as he spoke to her, "If there's room, I'll join you. But it's more urgent for you to get to shore safely."

As he spoke the words, he saw Joan scrunch and unscrunch her face, processing his words. He hadn't said anything any other gentleman wouldn't have suggested. Yet he could still see her bewildered expression.

"I'll be fine. I can swim. It's not far." He dismissed the questions he could see forming in her eyes and turned back to Jacob who was quickly rowing toward them.

By the time Jacob reached their boat, James had secured the oars so they couldn't drift away while they made the transition.

"I'll hold the boats together," James instructed. "Jacob, you help her into your boat."

"What can *I* do?" Sally asked, about to stand up.

"You can just sit there," James said urgently. If Sally even moved a bit it could throw the whole balance of the boat off and instead of James swimming, it would be Joan.

When a small pout formed under Sally's furrowed brow, he added, "We need someone to stabilize the boat."

That seemed to appease her, so slowly, Joan lifted herself into the other boat. Even in this small crisis situation he noticed how she moved with intention and grace.

The second Joan was in place, James checked where the leak had sprung. Damn. There was still too much weight in the boat. Water was seeping in.

"James, it's your turn," Jacob said, hand extended.

James eyed the rowboat. It was already looking crowded. As Joan shuffled to make room for him, the boat teetered.

"I'll be fine. I'll just row this boat back."

"Don't be silly. There's plenty of room. Jump in and we'll drag the other boat back," Jacob said.

Warily, James surveyed the boat again. If Jacob thought it would work, he wanted to trust the fellow. Make him look good in front of Sally.

Steadying himself in his boat, he gingerly lifted one leg to plant in the other boat.

Unfortunately, at the same time he stood flamingo-style in his rowboat, Sally took that opportunity to shift back saying, "I'll just make more room for you here."

And that shuffle was enough to rock their boat away from James's impending foot plant.

It was as if it were happening in slow motion. James watched the edge of the rowboat slip away, out from under his foot. Jacob stood strong in the center to balance his boat of ladies, and Joan was kneeling (again!), reaching out to him.

He was falling into her. The momentum was too much. His

head collided with her, but somehow it was only her mouth that crashed into his eye. Then—

SPLASH!

Down into the refreshingly cold water James went.

"James!"

He could hear the screaming from underwater. Thankfully he had shucked his jacket and waistcoat before going under. Swimming in clothing weighed a man down. Heaven forbid a lady fall in with all her layers.

Despite the screaming, and the shock of the water, James was calm. He had already resigned himself to swimming, so when he popped his head out of the water, he flicked his head, spraying water at whoever was waiting for him (he hoped he landed a few droplets on Joan), and belted out a laugh.

It was meant to be. "It's a good day for a swim, wouldn't you agree, Joan?"

A SHORT WHILE later, Joan was waiting for James on the shore. As per the selfless plan of James, she was completely safe and dry. Jacob and Sally had gone ahead to call for a towel and request tea to warm James up. It was a sunny day, but inside James might have a chill. Joan had opted to wait for him, just to be sure he didn't need any assistance.

James wasn't too far behind them, but swimming and pushing the boat had delayed him a bit.

Joan had offered to pull the boat, but James insisted on pushing it, saying he needed the exercise.

When James came nearer, she watched as he found the water shallow enough to stand in. With each step, he slowly revealed more of his body. A chiseled body that she could clearly see through a translucent white shirt. A body rippling with muscle that she couldn't tear her gaze away from. One hand rested on the boat as he stood for a moment, The other hand raked through his hair, spraying droplets everywhere. Water sluiced down his chest, down toward…she dared not look. But then she did.

His legs were powerful, thick thighs. Clearly he exercised frequently and it paid off. And she wanted to throw herself at him. It was silly. He was fine. The entire time he was fine. There wasn't even any danger in what he had just done. All the same, she was relieved he was fine and that he was back. And that he was wet.

Well, the wetness was just an observation. Not something she was particularly grateful for. Though…when she took a second look down over his body, she wasn't not grateful for him being so wet.

And oddly, she felt a bit…wet. Between her legs. A liquid pooling that she had never experienced before. And her nipples were hardening, like beacons, pointing to James. Almost exactly like a lighthouse, directing him to her. Calling him hither.

God, she needed to clear her head. She was beginning to sound like Mimi and all her fantasies.

"I'm glad you're back," she said, feeling she needed to say something, and that was so much safer than anything else that was floating around in her head.

"Missed me?" he teased back.

She rolled her eyes. It was natural for a duke to be arrogant, often to a fault. Typically Joan's experience with dukes was that their haughtiness was condescending, leaving only peons in their wake. But James's arrogance was different. He was self-assured but light. Always lifting up those around him. He knew who he was. No apologies. It was different for ladies of the *ton*. Joan knew who she was, but she had to hide much of it. Like the dagger she always kept on her person, always tucked away beyond her right-side pocket where she left a small gap for easy access.

James was moving again, honing in on her like she was a beacon. Pushing the boat ashore, he grunted.

Ugh. The deep, reverberating sound shot right to her core,

like a jolt. Her eyes flew wide. What was that reaction? It was like she no longer knew or understood her body. It was communicating in a foreign language.

When James plopped himself on the grass, he patted the spot beside him.

"Don't you want to change?" she asked, taking in his dripping translucent shirt. Pectoral muscles rippled with his movements, and all he was doing was shifting his legs so that his forearms rested atop his knees. Her eyes wanted to drift down to his breeches where she was sure she might see fabric clinging to...him. Beyond terrified to give in, she held his gaze instead.

"In a minute," he huffed.

And God, his shallow breaths were doing something to her. Parts of her body were zinging. Those parts of her body were shouting at her. Sending her a message loudly and clearly. *Danger.* She should leave. Temptation was growing. But she didn't want to go.

"We need to talk."

Oh dear, that didn't sound good.

"You need to tell me what's going on."

How did he know something was going on with her? Of course, they had so far been able to communicate effortlessly, like he was in tune with her somehow. But could he really sense her body's physical response to him? She wasn't close enough to him for him to feel her heat, was she? Were those zinging sensations visible?

She managed to keep her face still, and blandly asked, "What do you mean?"

"I didn't see Sally's reaction. What happened in the boat? Are we making progress with them?"

"Oh," she exhaled in relief, "that. It couldn't have gone better if we had planned it that way. Sally's eyes were dreamily focused on Jacob. And I'm quite sure I heard Sally exclaim, *My hero,* when he helped me enter the boat. I don't think she even noticed when you fell in the water."

At that, James barked out a laugh. The sound brought a quick smile to her own lips.

"Thanks for saving me." Despite James looking slightly incompetent amidst the rowboat transaction, she wanted him to know that she saw his efforts and appreciated him.

"Yes. About that…

"You could have done a better job saving me in return."

She could feel the intense heat under her jaw, crawling up into her cheeks. "And a gentleman wouldn't remind me of that obviously awkward encounter."

He chuckled.

Joan waved the topic away. "Anyway…I think Sally's smitten. And did you see where they were coming from? Behind those tall cattails so no one could see them. And did you see what she looked like after we called them over?"

"The hair?" James smirked.

"The lips?"

"Jacob's grin?"

The two chuckled together.

"I never thought Sally was the type," Joan mumbled.

With a waggle of his brows, James teased, "Every lady is the type."

"Not *every* lady," Joan countered, but not too vehemently.

"You've never…?"

For some reason, that question triggered something in her. Joan almost wished she had let a man take her to a private place and kiss her. That way she wouldn't feel so embarrassed that she was apparently not like *every* lady. But when James's eyes softened and she saw something flare in them, her heart fluttered.

"Well…it sounds like we did our job then," James stated.

And as much as that phrase should delight Joan, a small sadness crept into her heart. Or somewhere close. If Sally and Jacob were now attached, there was no reason for Joan and James to be attached.

"Why the frown?" James prodded.

"Oh, no reason." But she had a reason. If she was willing to admit it. She had been enjoying her time with James. He was funny. Carefree. Handsome…She didn't want to give him up just yet. "Perhaps Sally and Jacob just need one more push?"

James studied her face for a beat and said, "I couldn't agree more. We want to be absolutely sure that they'll become a couple."

"It's settled then. One more push?"

"Just a little nudge," he agreed as he bumped his shoulder into hers.

"Then we had better make it worthwhile."

"I couldn't agree more," he smiled.

She smiled.

There. That felt better.

CHAPTER ELEVEN

*"Bravery without forethought, causes a man to fight blindly
and desperately like a mad bull. Such an opponent, must not be
encountered with brute force, but may be lured into an ambush
and slain."*
—*Sun Tzu*

THE EVENING COULDN'T come fast enough, but before evening could come, afternoon tea had to take place. Joan almost skipped it, heading straight to her room, but she didn't want to appear an ungrateful guest. So she reminded herself that all she had to do was make polite conversation for a short while, and then she could go rest. Rest held a flexible definition for her, seeing how eager she was for this evening. She was bubbling with anticipation to trigger her and James's plan into action. It took everything in her to sit still and drink tea. But if anything could calm her nerves, tea should do the trick. And what was an hour or two of polite conversation? Nothing she couldn't do in her sleep. She was trained to be a lady.

Despite her invigorating pep talk, she was still feeling a bit anxious as she sipped at her tea while Countess Linsgate chatted with her.

At first the conversation touched only on safe topics. Weather. Current needlepoint projects. Favorite tea. Nothing to bat an eye at. All conversations she had actually had in her sleep. Though maybe more accurate to say, all conversations that could put her to sleep.

But then the countess asked coyly, "How was it out on the pond this afternoon?"

Joan wasn't sure which rumors had already been disseminated, and she certainly didn't want to add to them. Best to keep the events close to her chest. "It was a lovely afternoon. Though I do wonder what the weather is like in Copenhagen at this time of the year."

Countess Linsgate looked suitably stunned. "Copenhagen? I'm sure I don't know what it's like there right now."

The statement had meant to ruffle her feathers enough to distract her, but more importantly, the code word Copenhagen had been used as a signal to her sisters.

"Have you been? To erm—Copenhagen?" the countess asked as if she were grasping at a question in the air around her.

"Copenhagen?" Joan repeated loudly, looking around trying to catch her sisters' eyes. "I've never been to *Copenhagen*." Emphasizing the word again finally caught Nobi's attention. Joan watched as Nobi eyed Mimi and mouthed *Copenhagen* to her. Then she sat back and waited for a moment.

Nobi approached with a smile—fake, but only Joan could tell that. Using the most mellifluous tones, her elder sister asked, "I beg your pardon, Countess, but may we borrow Joan? We need her to settle a dispute for us?"

"Of course." The countess nodded her head. Likely only too grateful to not have to continue the discourse on Copenhagen.

Mimi took Joan's hand and the sisters sat at the perimeter of the group, not easily overheard by others.

"Copenhagen?" Mimi asked with a lifted brow and a slight smile playing on her face. "We haven't had to use that code word in a while."

Joan exhaled in relief. She could always count on her sisters. "I thought I could manage the small talk, but I needed a break."

"Happens to the best of us," Mimi said. "A woman can only endure so many conversations about fashion and food."

Nobi chuckled. "I happen to like those discussions."

"Do you? Or do you just play along to get along?" Mimi challenged lightly.

"It's a moot point. Joan needs us. What's going on?" Nobi turned to Joan, laying a hand on her forearm. "Are you all right?"

"I'm fine." Now that she had her sisters' attention, she wasn't sure how much she wanted to disclose.

"Well, you must be feeling good about yourself?" Mimi asked Joan after taking a sip of tea.

"Why do you say that?"

Mimi tilted her head at Sally who was staring off at a wall with a family portrait, the dreamy eyes clearly not taking in the familial features of their host.

"She looks like she's in love," Nobi said quietly.

And if anyone would know, it was Nobi. She had been pining after Chris since forever. But Joan asked anyway, "Do you really think so?"

Nobi nodded. "She has definitely changed since the ball when all the talk started."

Joan was feeling giddy at the success of her recent efforts. "She just needs one more small nudge."

"I don't think so. She looks like she's fallen—oomph." Nobi rubbed her upper arm and glared at Mimi. "What—"

"Yes," Mimi interrupted her sister. "What makes you think she needs another push?"

"James and I agreed that with one more little nudge, the fate of those two will be sealed."

Nobi opened her mouth but no words came out. Instead, words from Mimi filled the silence. "We couldn't agree more, could we Nobi?"

Nobi massaged her upper arm again. "Right," she murmured. "I just hope you two know what you're doing," she added as she reached for a tea biscuit.

"Of course we do. We have a plan."

"Ooooh," Mimi sing-songed. "What's the plan?"

Joan paused. She didn't really want to tell her sisters about the tryst they had planned for Jacob and Sally. It felt like a breach of trust to share the secret plan with her sisters. Then again, her sisters were her closest allies. She should trust them above anyone else. So…why didn't she want to in this instance?

"Come on, Joan. Tell us," Nobi pried.

Joan inched forward on her seat. Leaning forward, she poured herself another cup of tea while the ladies of the house party chatted around them, oblivious to the benevolent plans being shared in their midst.

"Well," she hesitated, and her sisters inched closer. "I'll tell you this." Her eyes darted back and forth between her sisters. "We have plans for them to seal their courtship with a kiss out in the gardens tonight."

Joan watched as Mimi's eyes widened in delight in direct correlation to the narrowing of Nobi's eyes.

"Are you sure that's a good idea?" Nobi asked cautiously.

"It's a marvelous idea," Mimi spoke over her sister in glee. "How can we help?"

"Now that you mention it, we don't want them to be caught. We just want them to have a moment alone together."

"We?"

"James and I." Joan gave Mimi a curious look. It should have been obvious whom she was referring to. She had just told her sisters that she and James were planning it.

"We?" Mimi mimicked in subdued tones to Nobi.

Nobi ignored her. "Do you think it's wise?"

"It's the perfect plan. James will get Jacob to the garden, and I'll direct Sally to the garden. Then the two of them can share a kiss."

"Or more." Mimi smiled.

"Mimi!"

"No need to scold me, Nobi."

"Someone has to if Boudicca is away." Nobi looked flushed, and a bit frumpled. But whether that was at the comment about more than kissing or having to chastise Mimi, Joan wasn't certain.

"They won't do more than kiss," Joan reassured them both. "Sally is too shy for that. Far too conservative to do more than a little kiss."

"Love makes people do crazy things," Nobi sighed.

"Not in this case," Joan said.

"How can you be sure?" Nobi asked.

"I know Sally."

"Would you have ever predicted that she would be so forward with James?"

"Well…" Joan would have never predicted that Sally would have acted that way. "But that was different."

Mimi only raised her eyebrows in question.

"That was not scandalous. At least, not *so* scandalous. This is different. She won't do anything more than kiss. Even a kiss might be a long shot."

Mimi and Nobi both offered a noncommittal, "Hmm…" in reply.

And really, that should have been a warning flag to Joan. But it wasn't.

HOURS LATER, THAT evening, Joan stood in the garden waiting for Sally to show up. She was hiding, backed up close to the roses where she could smell their delicate fragrance. The plan had been to tell Sally to meet Joan there, while James told Jacob to meet him there. In reality, neither Joan nor James would show their faces. The two starry-eyed lovers would meet and share a kiss, sealing their fate.

James would arrive any second so that they could be sure Jacob and Sally met up as planned. Joan's heart was racing. Her palms were clammy, and she could feel a bead of sweat dripping down the small of her back. In a few minutes, she and James would witness the final results of all of their efforts, and she felt as though she were floating on air. Bouncing from cloud to cloud, able to reach out and touch the stars.

From her side, a rustle sounded and then a voice whispered, "Are they here yet?" The gentle puff from his lips was close to her ear, and tickled her skin. A shiver danced down her spine like a ballerina.

She couldn't turn to look at him. "Not yet. They should arrive any minute now. What took you so long?"

"I couldn't get away. Were you waiting long?" It was a simple, innocent question, yet it sounded teasing.

"Not too long," she whispered. But another chill caused her body to tremble.

"Here, take my coat. You're cold." His large, warm hands ran up and down her upper arms before he slid out of his coat and wrapped it around her again. Did the man only wear a coat to offer it to others? It smelled divine, his heavy cologne enveloping her. At one time she had thought the cologne too strong, now it was heady. Protective.

He stood beside her. "Won't they be able to see us from here?"

"Won't the shadows hide us?"

"I don't think so. Let's not take that chance. We don't want them too angry with us. Come on." He entwined his fingers with hers and tugged her behind the roses. There was just enough space for two bodies to hide between the roses and the wall behind them. James leaned against the wall and pulled Joan's back to his chest.

"Shhh…" he hissed, latching his arm around her waist. Even though she hadn't been speaking, Joan clamped her mouth shut. They could hear footsteps.

But then she couldn't help herself, she turned her head back slightly and whispered, "I'm quite excited." And she was. Her heart was almost hammering outside of her chest. She wanted all the happiness, security, and good reputation for her friend as possible. This was the moment that could seal everything.

"As am I," came an altogether too close whisper. "But we must be quiet now." One of James's hands ribboned up her front and then his index finger touched her lips.

And that's when the red flag waved. It waved blindingly right in front of her face. The largest flag she had ever borne witness to.

Her body stiffened.

She was alone with a man—a rake. She was pressed against his body—in the dark. In a garden. Alone. His finger had just brushed her lips. And her lips burned from his soft touch. What the deuce was she doing here? This was a terrible idea. She could have sent Sally out to the garden and left it at that. Why did she need to be there to witness it? If Sally was going to kiss Jacob, why did she need to witness that?

God, why had none of these questions surfaced earlier? How had her sisters let her go through with this asinine plan?

Before Joan could even begin to defend herself to logic, the voices started. And her plans went from terrible to mortifying.

Joan couldn't make out everything that Jacob and Sally were saying, thankfully they were speaking in hushed tones and they were just far enough away from them. But—

Oh God, what was that sound? A moan.

Followed by a groan.

A mewl.

And then an "Oh God, Jacob."

Oh God, Joan! Joan. The cautious one. The one with a level head. The one who made calculated decisions based on reason and common sense. And don't forget etiquette. What the deuce had happened? She had met a rake and let him influence her. That's what had happened. And now she stood here, eyes squeezed shut, wishing there was a way to squeeze her ears shut as well.

And how could she turn off her nipples? They were hard as pebbles. And tensing. And that spot between her legs. How could she turn down the throbbing there?

She felt James's body harden behind her.

She squeaked, and a large, warm hand flew to her mouth.

"Shhh…" James hissed. And she could hear the tension in his voice.

And all Joan could think was, *what does James think about all of this right now?* He can't surely be as calm as he feels.

CHAPTER TWELVE

"The wise warrior avoids the battle."
—*Sun Tzu*

WHAT THE HELL had he been thinking? This plan was a terrible idea. Who the devil had come up with it? James was inwardly shaking his head. He couldn't recall who had suggested the tryst. Or who had recommended that they both wait out in the garden to ensure the tryst happened. Who had picked the hiding place? Why did this have to happen at night? Darkness hid many things, but not a swelling cock building against the backside of the heat-emanating woman pressed into him.

James would have to be absolutely delirious to think Joan didn't feel his hardness pushing into her bottom, but he couldn't do anything about it. There was no wiggle room. Well, there was some wiggle room if he wanted to be honest about it. Wiggling room. Grinding room. Ahem—but there was no room to wiggle away from her. The best he could do was try to think of conjugating Latin verbs or regurgitating math formulas. But for the life of him, he couldn't think of one. What even was Latin? Math? Numbers, right?

"I'm sorry," he whispered softly into her ear.

And perhaps that was the wrong thing to do because he felt her shiver. And that small shiver shook her all the way down her spine and settled into a jiggle of her bottom. Which, as he was all too well aware, was resting snuggly around his throbbing cock.

And he shouldn't do it, because really, based on what just happened, another whisper didn't make the most sense, yet he did it anyway, "Don't move, Joan." If she moved too much he was afraid he was going to embarrass himself.

Another shiver. Another jiggle. A thicker cock. A groan from the back of his throat.

The once-thought-to-be chilly night air was growing thick and hot. He could feel Joan's bosom inhaling and exhaling, nearly panting, just above his forearm. What he wouldn't do to raise his arm to feel the underside of her breasts. Even clothed, he knew he would revel in their heaviness.

But he was using all of his self-control to remain a statue. If he could just hold it together while Sally and Jacob kissed. Oh God, they were moaning louder now. James could hear the rustling of fabric being hitched up. It was difficult to see what was happening through the rose bushes, but he could see Jacob lifting Sally. And he was pretty sure her legs were wrapped around his friend's waist now. And...nope...he didn't want to admit it, but it really did look like Jacob's breeches were pooled at his feet. And...oh, yes...there was some grunting and... devil take it...thrusting action. Yes, that was definitely happening.

There was no denying it.

When James and Joan had discussed the innocence of a shared kiss between Sally and Jacob, they were excited for the couple. Not as excited as the couple was currently displaying, but giddy that love might bloom. Well, yes, something was blooming right now. James didn't particularly want to identify the number of thickening cocks in the vicinity, and he could only hope that Joan had her eyes (and somehow her ears) shut so that she didn't—

And then the unthinkable happened. Joan's hand grasped his– desperately. He could feel the tension in her grip. Panic. But a controlled panic. And slowly, inch by inch, she drew his hand up to her breast. He knew what she was doing but couldn't believe it was actually happening. She was initiating something with him. Something sensual. And he wanted it. The desperation emitted from her clinging hand was a reflection of the desperation he felt in his heart—no, not his heart. His…well, definitely his cock. He wanted this woman, and he was about to have her. If he let her take control. He inhaled a ragged breath and softly exhaled in anticipation. His fingers were a hair's width away from her breasts. Breasts that he didn't want to admit he had dreamt of last night. Massaging those creamy mounds. Licking. Nipping. Sucking her nipples into his mouth. Those had just been innocent—all right, not so *innocent*, but they hadn't been a reality, so they were innocent enough. And now his dreams were coming true. If he let her…

He thought for the second time, he could let her, or he could stop her. If he stopped her, he might never know the weight of her breasts, the curve of them. The shape. If instead he let her move his hands, everything might change. Then again, it didn't have to change. She knew he was a rake…so she knew what she was getting into. Continuing the debate in his mind, while his fingers were tempted to dig into the front of her ribs, he landed on the argument that would seal his fate.

If he denied her this, she would feel rejected. And he would never want to hurt her. He never wanted her to feel the sting of rejection. What he knew of Joan was that she was a lady. An innocent. And here she was, finding courage to make a move. He could never deny her that.

So he let her.

The second his palm cupped her breast, he felt her body melt into him. His head fell back against the wall. Relief surged through him. Just to touch her. This indomitable, curious, cautious woman who was not acting cautiously at all with him.

He wanted her to sink into him. He wanted to bear her weight. Her burdens. He wanted her to let him in…in every way.

But then she moaned. And the moan was just a little too loud to go unnoticed.

"Joan, you must be quiet."

"Don't stop," she mumbled.

"I couldn't even if I wanted to, but you must be quiet. Can you be a good girl and do that for me, Joan?" He lightly pinched her nipple to test her.

A muffled moan caught in her throat, and she nodded.

"That's what I thought," he whispered in her ear. Not holding back now. He let his breath rush in her ear while waiting for her body to tremble. "That's a good girl," he said, soothing her quivering body. With one hand on her breast and one still covering her mouth, he asked, "I'm going to use both of my hands on you now."

The back of her head pressed into his chest, nodding.

Before he indulged, he took one of her hands and brought it up behind his neck so she had a part of him to hang onto. To cling to. To dig her nails into. And she did just that kind of digging, the second he brought his hand to her breast and squeezed,

For sure, he thought she would moan too loudly, but he was proud of her when he saw her tighten her lips, sealing any sounds from escape. But when she arched her breasts into his hands, he almost lost control entirely.

He tugged on her bodice. When nothing happened, he growled quietly in disappointment. Not to be deterred, he dipped his finger into the bodice and pulled out one of her plump breasts. For a brief second, he thought he was going to come in his breeches at the sight of the most perfect breast he had ever seen. It was too dark to discern the exact color of her nipple, but he could see its turgid peak. And that pert nipple needed to be sucked.

He rolled her nipple between his fingertips, feeling himself harden even more.

"Joan," his hoarse words crawled through the air. "If you want more, turn around." Her body tensed, and he wasn't sure if he had scared her away. He had told himself that he only let her make her move because she was the one in control. And he could only hope this invitation to turn around wasn't removing that control from her hands. So he waited. He didn't nudge her at all. Just…waited.

And then gradually she turned around. Her head down, he couldn't read her emotions. He desperately wanted to tip her chin up to look at him, but he wanted her to have control. So he waited again. Finally, she inclined her head. And his breath caught in his throat.

A few loose locks of hair framed her face as half-lidded eyes lazily looked up at him. Not in embarrassment as he was loath to predict, but in desire. And that was all the encouragement he needed.

He pressed his back into the wall and sunk into a shallow squat, opening his legs for her to straddle. He lowered his head to her breast, pausing an inch from her nipple. He let out a soft breath, and looked up at her, licking his bottom lip. Waiting again.

With one hand she cradled her breast, with the other, she pulled the back of his neck toward her nipple.

He started with a soft lick. Then a flick of her nipple. When her head dropped back and she moved closer to him, he pulled her breast into his mouth.

A whimper threatened her lips, so he pulled away.

"I'll be quiet," she vowed, arching herself into him.

He lowered in his squat, finding her skirts and lifting them so that he could brace his hands on her hips. Then he lifted her to straddle him. Ye gods, he couldn't remember the last time he was this hard. The last time he had ever desired a woman in this way. To these depths.

"James," the soft pleading sound of his name on her lips was his undoing.

"How much do you want, Joan?" He wanted to give her everything. Whether that made him a cad or generous, he wasn't sure. Perhaps it made him both. Her body pressed into him. Her breath warming his skin. Her hands tantalizing him. He wanted to show her pleasure. Pleasure he knew she had never experienced. He would be her first. He would be the one to introduce her to a world that no man had ever—could ever—show her. She would call his name. Dig her nails into his skin. Writhe on his body. And right now, he wanted nothing more than everything with her.

And then a thought shook him.

He could be the first one.

Or.

He could be the only one.

His body quivered. The shock of the thought. The chill in the air. Her body's responsiveness to him. All of it. He thought he was ready for her answer, but when she spoke, his heart grew wings and fluttered rapidly in his chest.

"Give me pleasure, James." Her cheek was pressed to his, and her hands were affixed to his shoulders.

He gazed at her face. "Give me your lips, Joan."

She sighed, parting her lips and leaning into him. Slowly at first, he placed a gentle kiss to the corner of her mouth. But she tasted too sweet, emanated too much heat for him to go slow for long. His tongue tangled in her mouth exploring her. Discovering the depths of this complex woman. A woman who made him laugh, peaked his curiosity, and communicated so effortlessly with him. She was like nothing he had ever expected. What was he a green boy with no experience? But feeling this woman now, he sensed he had never really been with a woman before her.

And she was taking control again. Her body was rubbing against him, finding pleasure in the friction building between his cock and her slit.

The urgency was building. He could feel his pleasure pooling at the bottom of his spine and the tightening at the base of arousal. And he knew she was about to find the pleasure she had asked him for because she ripped her mouth from his and was rubbing her wet self on him. Her breasts bouncing in his face, he panted, "Take it, Joan. Be a good girl and come for me."

Her moans built until he didn't think he could take it anymore. She threw her head back and he nipped at the column of her neck. Wanting to mark her skin, he herded all of his self-control and held back, desperately needing to protect her from what scandal that mark might cause.

Her throaty groans blew life into his hardened heart. He could feel it—himself, his ice walls—melting under her heat. Heat from her body, but more than that, heat from her essence. Who she was. Joan. He wanted to own this heat. Access it whenever he needed it.

"James, what you're doing to me..."

She didn't finish the thought, only shifted and rubbed herself against him deeper. He had wanted more. Everything from her. But in this moment, he knew he couldn't handle that much of her. This. Her taking her pleasure and finding a new world with him. That was what he needed right now. The edges of his mind darkened at the amount of pleasure he absorbed from her.

And just when he knew she was about to find release, he covered her mouth again with his to stifle the sounds that would inevitably come out of her. That's what he told himself. But it was equally to muffle the groan that was being wrenched from his body as he felt his cock explode in his breeches.

CHAPTER THIRTEEN

"The whole secret lies in confusing the enemy, so that he cannot fathom our real intent."
—*Sun Tzu*

THE NEXT MORNING James woke from a restless sleep. It had been impossible to close his eyes without seeing Joan's face full of pleasure. Head lolled back, eyes half-lidded. And every time he closed his eyes and saw her experiencing that pleasure, a pang of lust shot down his back, up his legs, and met in the middle.

One visual from the dream stood out, and he knew he wouldn't be forgetting it anytime soon. He saw her dancing in his arms with a shimmering smile locked on her lips. They started in a ballroom, but in a flash they were in a bedroom. He couldn't be sure if it were his, but the bed was large. And then she was underneath him. Writhing. Her hair strewn about on the pillow, her eyes heavy, almost closed, just as they had been in the garden. She was saying his name and he was hovering over her. Their clothes were in heaps around the room. With nothing on, he could feel her soft skin against him everywhere. He was hard. Throbbing. And she was arching up into him. He was restlessly edging closer to her entrance. She was saying something to him, pleading, and just before he could respond, the dream vanished.

When he awoke, his cock had been pressed up against his pillow. Hard. Aching. The need for her was driving him. Compelling him. Energizing him. Remembering her passion and responsiveness caused his arousal to swell.

He rolled over onto his back and palmed himself. He gripped the base of his cock and pulled up in one smooth motion. He groaned in partial relief, the sound extending his length. Knowing the pleasure he could have, he closed his eyes and imagined her. His goddess.

Envisioning her smile. Her laughter. He recalled her quirky interests. Her passion for people. And daggers. It brought a smile to his own face, and he started pumping harder. Base to tip. Back down. Base to tip. He could feel precum on his tip. Clenching his jaw. Pleasure pooling in his spine. The warmth of her brown eyes overtook his vision and heated his heart. He gripped himself harder. One hand played with his balls while the other tugged up and down.

Tightening at the base of his cock. Heat flooding his groin. Pleasure throttling his limbs.

Two more pumps.

White-hot pleasure ripped through him. A ragged breath left his body.

He was sated, but not relieved. It was nothing like being with her in person. And last night in the garden had been like nothing he had ever felt before. Joan.

She was beautiful. Considerate. Intelligent. And so damn responsive to his touch. Just thinking of her made his cock twitch, and he had just taken care of himself. But it hadn't been enough. He wanted her. Yet not as a wife. He was not made to love or be loved. He knew that too well. His mother had made sure to instill that lesson in him. A man was made for two purposes: provide and procreate.

His father had provided food, shelter, and security. James's basic needs had been met his whole life, so his mother endlessly reminded him. And now it was his turn to procreate and provide. Only, James had no interest in perpetuating the lifeless cycle.

There had been no affection, not even a hint of it, from his parents. Love (if one could call it that) was defined as meeting needs. Keeping family a satisfied. His parents had contained him in a bubble. Riding slow horses and being cautious around everyone. Everywhere. Danger lurked behind every bush. Only family could be trusted, and hardly them. For his eighteenth birthday, he had received the one and only gift his parents ever gave him. Weren't their daily provisions enough? The gift was a book called *The Art of War* written by Sun Tzu. James abhorred it with everything in his being, yet he kept it to remind himself of the *love* his parents had for him. Of course, he had rebelled. Fast, faster, and the fastest horses were all he rode. He lived for a dare. To be reckless.

And no, he would not provide, nor would he procreate, for anyone. This life he had he would live only for himself. Love? Ha! He would have laughed in the face of love if he believed love had a face, or even existed at all.

So no, there was no such thing as love. There were complex feelings and lust.

That's how he knew that while he wanted Joan…there was no future for them. Lust never paved the way to a happily ever after. But maybe he could just see her again. There was no harm in being around her.

After the passion had settled last night, he wasn't sure what to expect from his dagger-wielding paramour. If he could call her that…

But all she had done was take a small step back (considering the confined space) and say, "Thank you. For th-that." He chuckled as he recalled her slight stutter and the way she had tucked her hair behind her ear. When he had tried to interrupt her, she halted him with a hand to his chest. It had stopped his words as well as his breath. That small delicate touch. And then she looked him dead in the eye and said, "We got caught up in the moment. I have no expectations."

Then, they had waited awkwardly (which was putting it lightly—it had in fact been *the* most awkward fifteen minutes of James's entire life) while Sally and Jacob finished dressing and talking and returned to the house. James and Joan had followed at a distance, and that was the night. What a night. James was still reeling.

And yet he needed to see her again. They were no longer in cahoots to seal Sally and Jacob's relationship. Clearly, all the sealing that needed to be sealed had been sealed last night. So in order to see her again, he had to be more clever.

Though if he were being honest with himself, clever was not his strongest attribute at the moment. His cleverness was so reflected in his conversation with Sam and Chris. He knew she liked to practice throwing her daggers at targets, so she had told him before. Knowing of one site for archery practice, that's where he was headed, but he didn't want to show up alone. That would be too obvious. Obvious of what…he wasn't sure. He just knew he never wanted to be so ostentatious.

So James stood outside the breakfast room waiting for his friends to exit. They should be out any minute.

"Duke?" A sultry voice greeted him.

He looked up into the smoldering eyes of Lady Whitney. It was still early in the morning, but if James had stopped to notice, the widow was radiating heat of the bedroom variety. He did no such thing though.

"Lady Whitney. Good morning." He tipped his head and looked away to dismiss the possibility of chatter—idle or otherwise. He was waiting for his friends.

"Do you have plans this early in the morning?" Her husky voice dropped in volume as she leaned in and stroked a finger up his forearm.

"Yes, thank you. Enjoy your morning." He really wasn't looking to have a conversation with anyone except Sam and Chris.

"Oh? Might I convince you to exchange your plans for something more tantalizing upstairs?"

"No, thank you." His eyes flickered over to the breakfast room door, to see Chris and Sam finally emerging. Realizing her hand was still on his forearm, he extracted her claws and moved toward his friends while Lady Whitney departed.

"What was that about?" Sam asked.

"Nothing," he answered, waving off the question.

"It didn't look like nothing," Chris chimed in.

"Was it nothing of importance or nothing of interest?" Sam pried.

James shook his head. "What's the difference?" He huffed, frustrated that his friends were so caught up on a moment in time that he had hardly noticed.

"Well," Sam slapped him on the back, "it looks as though the widow was propositioning you—which is of importance—and that you were rejecting her—which means she's nothing of interest."

"And?"

"You don't find that…important and interesting?" Sam asked with a light chuckle.

"What are you talking about?" Clearly vexed now, James furrowed his brow.

"It just seems that she's someone you would normally take up that offer with," Sam explained.

What was Sam talking about? Why was he so caught up on the widow? So what if he didn't want to bed her. It was early in the morning. It didn't signify.

"We should go for a walk." No other explanation needed. This was the reason he had been waiting for them. It was just a simple plan laid out before his friends.

Sam and Chris just stared at him as he made his pronouncement.

"Where are we off to?" Sam asked dubiously, as if he could already read into James's plan. Of course he couldn't.

"Nowhere in particular. Just need to get some fresh air and exercise. Don't be lazy."

"We weren't—" Chris started to say.

"No time to chat." Facing the two men, James flapped his

arms wide and clapped his hands down, one on each man's shoulders. "Let's go."

Sam offered half a smirk and Chris smiled casually. "I could use the air," Chris said.

"We could all use air. It's a known human dependency." Sam cracked a full smile now.

"Right then. Off we go." James almost winced at his last turn of phrase. Something he was pretty sure he had never said in that exact tone before. An altogether too high-pitched tone with uncredited eagerness. "I mean," he dropped his voice to a lower register, "let's get out of here."

Sam chuckled as James turned around to walk outside. James was pretty sure he heard Sam mumble something about twenty pounds to Chris. When he glanced back, Chris merely shrugged one shoulder and shook Sam's hand.

"What's that about?" James inquired.

"Nothing. Just an old bet," Sam said cagily.

"And you're not going to share that with me?"

"No." Sam sauntered ahead of him, mimicking, "Off we go!" which made Chris chuckle.

It only took a short time before James regretted bringing his friends along with him. Sam kept suggesting different turns or pathways to take. It was growing more and more difficult to nonchalantly demand that they all forge ahead in the direction James intended they take.

"I think this looks like a great path to take," Sam was saying again.

"That goes down to the stables." James had no idea where it led except that it was not to the archery targets. "Not interested in the stables," he mumbled as he ambled forward.

"I'd be curious to see their stables." Sam's voice was unusually optimistic.

James was growing more irritated by the second, so when he whirled around to Sam, his loud voice caused Sam to raise his hand defensively. "If anyone would be interested in seeing the stables it would be me. I'm not interested in them, ergo neither are you two."

"Not sure that's how that works," Chris added unhelpfully.

"Where are we going then? What are you interested in seeing?"

James's blood was boiling. Couldn't Sam just drop it and follow along for once in his life? "Nature. I just want to see some damn nature, all right? Now can we quit chatting like a bunch of mother hens and get on with it?"

"Huh. Never really thought I'd see the day…" Sam intentionally left the thought unfinished as he poked Chris in the arm. "Wasn't he just saying he would never?"

"Never, what? What are you talking about?"

"Nature," Sam said with a chuckle. "Show us more of this *nature* you want to see."

"Fine." James stomped onward. After emerging from a small copse of trees, James sighed in relief. A few yards away was Joan. His shoulders dropped in ease and a small smile played at his lips.

"Ahh….nature," Sam exhaled roughly as he extended both arms out to his sides. "The beauty of *nature* can't be beat."

"Drop it," James urged, only causing a low rumble of a laughter to emerge from Sam.

"You owe me twenty pounds," Sam called over his shoulder to Chris.

James stared straight ahead, but he heard the slap of hands and the exchange of money.

"It seems as though you can't stay away from *nature*. When did that happen?" Sam asked.

"I'm not sure what you mean." There was no point in denying Sam's question, but James didn't really want to process all of his thoughts at the moment. He just wanted to be around Joan again.

"I'm not sure who you're trying to fool, James. If you like the chit, just court her." This coming from Sam, the man who was also a self-proclaimed bachelor. The most competitive man James knew. So if he was planning to do something, he committed to it. He made it happen. There were very few times Sam didn't accomplish his goals. If he wanted to be a bachelor, then he would be one. If he wanted to interrogate James, he wouldn't stop until he got the answer he was looking for.

Despite the knowledge of Sam's persistence, James attempted to deflect him. "I can't do that," James finally answered. There was no way he would court Joan. She was a lady. He was a rake. She wanted love. He didn't even believe it existed. They weren't going to happen.

"Why not?" Chris asked.

"I'm never going to marry." Saying the words he had always said felt empty this time. For far too long he had believed that he couldn't have a family. Couldn't perpetuate the neglectful childhood he had experienced. And still, he couldn't imagine a wife, marriage, and children. But...something had shifted inside of him, leaving him frustrated.

"Then what are we doing here?" Sam challenged. James stared at his friend. A friend of too many years to count. And while he didn't exactly want to punch him in the mouth, he didn't exactly *not* want to either. It was one option to shut him up. But when James considered not only the bloody mess that would cause but also the unnecessary chaos, he opted out of punching.

"I have no idea. But since we're here..." James strolled toward the targets. Less of a stroll and more of a magnetic force drawing him, pulling him, relentlessly, toward Joan. What was it about her that he found so intriguing? Certainly her affinity for daggers could be part of it. And of course, her kisses from last night...

But every woman could kiss...though not like her. And not every woman had such an inclination toward blades. So blades it was.

Then, to pull himself out of the rabbit hole he was falling down, he bellowed, "Hello!" Anything to quit the current conversation he had been having with his friends and then with himself. His friends knew nothing. Didn't they know his past family life? He would make a terrible husband, never mind father.

He didn't want to think about the future he couldn't have. Wait. He meant, the future he didn't want to have. All he wanted to think of was Joan. And there she was. Nearly black hair, soft tresses escaping her coiffure, floating softly in the breeze. Her eyes flew to him in surprise. Her hand was raised with a dagger. Yes, that was very intriguing about her.

Especially considering that she was aiming at him.

CHAPTER FOURTEEN

*"The greatest strength lies not in physical might, but in the
strength of character."*
—Joan of Arc

THWACK!

Joan had just let her dagger fly. Hitting the target smack in the middle of the bullseye gave her a sense of relief. Accomplishment. Control. This was one of a few places where she felt fully alive and herself. She had also been feeling that way with James lately, but she was trying to push those thoughts out of her mind. Her sisters understood her, and she knew she could always be herself around them. She was lucky to have them, though in this moment she was missing Boudicca. One day they might all be married and the family dynamics would change entirely. Joan hadn't given that future thought much consideration until now, noting the impact of Boudicca's absence.

How would she manage the changing dynamic? Would she have a husband? Would he fit in well with her sisters? It was hard to imagine. So instead, she threw another dagger.

"Nice throw," Mimi cheered.

Nobi clapped softly beside her, warming up to throw her set next. Even though knife throwing was Joan's strength, her sisters engaged in the activity. Over the years, Joan had provided some pointers so that each sister could throw a blade with decent accuracy. Given that it was Joan's passion, she practiced more often and out threw her sisters every time. Today was no exception.

She and her sisters were eccentric. Joan knew that. The four sisters grew up quite aware of their precarious reputation. It was safe. Of that there was no doubt. They were invited to balls, routs, house parties, and the like. But Joan always felt that one wrong move could ruin them. Now that Boudicca had married Wes, it gave them an extra layer of security. Him being a duke and all.

A duke.

Joan wanted to throw another dagger. The damn duke dare. It was weighing on her mind again. How could it not after her…encounter…with James?

Never, ever, ever did she ever act so recklessly as she did last night. And never, ever, ever had she expected herself to have any…feelings…for him.

"Joan,"—Nobi cleared her throat—"are you all right?"

"Hmm? Why?" Joan asked distractedly. Usually knife throwing focused her mind, but it felt as though she were thinking in a cloud. Only the bullseye looked clear.

"You're petting your blade…weirdly," Nobi answered.

Joan looked down at her fingers, startled to see her irregular actions. Her fingers were grazing the engraved portion which made her blades a unique set. Each blade had a different quote from Joan of Arc. It was not only fitting, but inspiring.

"There's no *normal* way to pet a blade, Nobi." Mimi's voice commanded attention. "What happened last night between you and James, Joan?"

"What? Why would you think anything happened last night?" Obviously Joan was feigning ignorance. As much as she loved her sisters, she just wasn't ready to share anything yet.

Mimi flicked her finger down, pointing at the blade. "You're petting that blade. Weirdly—as Nobi said. And as much as I know you like to throw daggers, I don't think I've ever quite seen this level of angst in you before. So spill it. What happened?"

"Nothing happen—"

"Joan." Mimi's hands were on her hips and Nobi had her shoulders pulled back, as if she were bracing herself for the news.

"You can tell us, we won't judge you. We're your sisters."

"That's exactly why you might judge me, Nobi." Joan sighed. It was futile to feign ignorance.

"I kissed him." But she wasn't a fool. She wasn't about to share everything.

Mimi grasped her hands, deftly avoiding the pointy blade. "Oooooh. Tell us everything."

That would not be happening.

"We kissed. That's all there is to say—"

Mimi interrupted, "There's more. There must be more. This is James we're talking about—"

"That's all there is to say." Joan put her foot down. Literally. A small puff of dust wafted above her slippered foot to prove it. She hoped it was having the dramatic effect she desired.

"Mimi, that's all she wants to say. Let's respect her privacy."

An exaggerated huff came out of Mimi's nostrils. "Fine." She crossed her arms over her chest. "What's the plan now?"

"The plan?" Joan echoed. "There is no plan. We kissed. It was nice. That's all."

"It was nice?" Mimi narrowed her eyes at Joan. Then, quite contrary to her usual over the top pronouncements, she said in a hushed tone, "Lies."

"Lies? I beg your pardon?"

And then more true to Mimi's style, she shouted, "Lies!"

Joan glanced around, even though she was quite sure they were alone. Seeing no one, yet all the same she shushed her sister. "Mimi, please. Keep your voice down."

"Only if you tell the truth."

Well, the truth was not going to be revealed. Joan did not exactly want to share all of her truths. That it wasn't just a nice kiss. It was a perfect kiss. A slice of heaven. With the gravity of the place too. Her feet felt as though they had been floating on air. And then when James had lifted her to straddle his hips. She was undone.

"Why are you fanning yourself? It's not that hot out," Mimi broke into her thoughts.

"It grew rather warm in the last few minutes. Wouldn't you agree, Nobi?"

Nobi looked at each of her sisters. Mimi throwing daggers with her eyes, and Joan pleading silently. With no winning option, Nobi shrugged.

"Just how *nice* was the kiss?" Mimi teased.

"It was very nice." Life changing. Enough to ruin her for all other men. But that didn't matter. James was not to be hers. He didn't want to be a husband. And she most certainly did not want to snag a husband who would spend his life resenting the role.

"Would you like to do it again?"

Really, there was no point refusing that. "Yes." But she also wanted to clarify the situation to her sisters. "But I won't."

"Why not?" Nobi asked with widened eyes.

"You think I should?" Nobi was a voice of reason between the three of them. If she were doubting Joan's decision, her ears were listening.

"If you liked it…why not?" Nobi suggested quietly.

"We're ladies. We have our reputations to worry about," Joan replied.

Mimi was waving her hands in the air dismissively. "Just don't let anyone find out. Wait. Did someone see you two? I didn't hear anything. Nobi, did you hear any gossip?"

Nobi pursed her lips together and shook her head.

"You weren't caught, were you?"

"No." Joan could feel her heart rate picking. Of course she would love to kiss him again. She would love a lot from him, things she didn't even know she wanted. She could feel it. But he was not available to her, and that was the most vexing part of all of this. If he could just be open to the idea of marriage, maybe she wouldn't have any qualms about trapping him into the holy matrimony. She really, really, really wanted to throw that dagger about now. She raised her voice as she answered Mimi again, "No. We weren't caught. But we could have been. And that's reason enough to stay away from the rake." As her voice rose, so did her knife-wielding hand.

And then a loud, booming voice called out, "Hello!"

She whirled around, knife high in the air, to see the rake himself.

"Speaking of being together," Mimi teased. "There's your rake now."

"Quiet," Joan hissed.

"Ummm…Joan, perhaps you want to lower your weapon," Nobi whispered loudly.

"Yes. Quite right, Nobi." Joan placed her dagger on the barrel they had been using as a table and watched as the Betting Buddies less one made their way over.

"Afternoon, ladies," Sam called out. Once they were near, Sam asked, "Don't you ladies look lovely. Chris, don't you think Nobi looks lovely?" Sam poked Chris in the ribs as Chris awkwardly stared at Nobi.

When Chris said nothing, Sam poked him again.

"Uh…yes, you look lovely Nobi. As always," Chris admitted reluctantly. And was that a small blush Joan could see creeping up his neck?

Well, that was awkward. But Joan didn't have a moment to analyze that interaction.

Same spoke up again, "What a perfect day for a competition."

"You say that about every day," Chris ribbed him.

"And it is true of every day." Sam rubbed his hand over his mouth. "Now what do we have here? Dagger throwing? What kind of wagers can we place on this?"

"Place wagers all you like, so long as you don't mind losing to a woman," Mimi stated the obvious, as was obvious to all three sisters. "Oh that's right. You're quite comfortable losing to women, aren't you?"

"Don't poke the bear." Amused, Chris stepped in offering advice.

"He's nothing but a stuffed bear. All soft on the inside," Mimi teased.

Sam stood to his full height, saying, "There's nothing soft about me, and I have no problems proving that to you."

"Please do—" Mimi was interrupted quickly by Chris.

"There'll be no proving any hardness here. There. Or any-where."

"Not on Old MacDonald's Farm either," Mimi taunted. "E-I-E-I-O."

"You're just a child," Sam scoffed. "Although I don't usually permit it, I don't mind allowing a child the upper hand in a competition. It boosts their confidence. What say you to a five-yard advantage? You may throw the first dagger."

Mimi glared at him. "You bet your arse I'll throw the first dagger. I'll throw it right at your—"

"Enough," Chris stepped in at the same time as Nobi. Each one calming their corresponding friend.

"Shall we walk this off, Mimi?" Nobi asked gently.

"I'm fine," Mimi shook her sister's hand from her shoulder, then stalked off back toward the house.

Sam belted out a laugh which only caused Mimi to vocalize a loud growl.

Joan wasn't even sure how it all happened, but once her sisters took off, so did Chris and Sam; thus leaving her alone with James.

Exactly where she wanted to be.

But not.

"You mentioned you liked daggers. I don't think I quite real-ized the extent of it. It's rather an obsession for you, isn't it?" James was standing a foot away, dark hair gleaming in the sun, eyes shining, smile even brighter. Was there an ounce of this man that wasn't sparkling right now?

"Right after family, they're my life."

"Nice to hear you have your priorities aligned. Not every family does."

And that, right there, that remark, reminded her of some subtle comments James had made before. And she thought to herself that now might be the perfect time to press him for details.

"Did your family?"

It was a direct question. More direct, more personal than any she had yet to ask him. But she had nothing to lose. If he didn't answer her, she was no better off than having not asked the question. And if he was upset with her, well, it wasn't as if anything was going to happen between them anyway. And if he did answer the question…well, she really hadn't thought that far ahead. That would be a miracle—

"No."

"What?"

He stepped closer. The air around her—the vast expanse of air mind you—shrunk. As if she couldn't breathe in his presence. And he wasn't even that close. He was still an arm's length away. And she was quite familiar with the length of his arms now…so really, she knew that to be a fact.

"You asked if my family had their priorities straight. I answered, no."

"Oh. I'm sorry to hear that."

"It's in the past." He shrugged, but it didn't really look like a casual shrug. It didn't shrug the invisible weight from his shoulders like it was a feather, more like it was a ton of bricks and his shoulders were struggling to heave off the burden.

"Is it in the past, truly?" And she knew she shouldn't ask her next question, but something about being in James's vicinity made her reckless, so she went with it. "Or is it affecting your future too much?"

Another shrug.

"I have to go." He turned to leave.

"I'm sorry. I shouldn't have asked."

"Perhaps not. But it's fine." He smiled. "What I meant was, I have to go water some plants."

"Right now? Which plants?" That was completely unexpected. She had no clue what he was talking about. "We're at a house party a little bit busy at the moment, wouldn't you say? What plants could you possibly have to water?"

He was laughing at her with his eyes now. "You'll figure it out. I'll return shortly. Don't go anywhere." And with that, he took off into the bushes.

As she watched the trees soak him into their branches, she noticed his hands working on something at the front of his breeches.

Oh. That kind of watering. Well, she felt rather foolish.

She took up a dagger, readied her stance, and flung it toward the target. Bullseye.

Taking another dagger, she inhaled deeply, and was about to launch when—

"Eeeyaaaa!" A loud screech rattled through the trees up into the clear blue sky.

"James?!" she shouted, running toward the sound. What could have possibly happened to the man? She ran into the grove, calling his name. "James!"

"Joan, stop." James bellowed. "Don't move."

"Where are you?" Joan looked around wildly. She could hear him but she couldn't see him anywhere.

"I'm over here."

"I can't see you—"

"Look up."

And there hung James in a tree, caught up in a hunter's snare by one foot. His hair hung down at all angles, a flush was in his cheeks. But what really grabbed her attention was his hand on his partially exposed cock, falls flapping in the light breeze.

CHAPTER FIFTEEN

"Thus the expert in battle moves the enemy, and is not moved
by him."
—*Sun Tzu*

"JOAN?" JAMES'S VOICE beckoned to her. "Might you be willing
to rescue a poor fellow?"

She chuckled. He looked a bit adorable hanging from the
tree. Vulnerable. Something he had yet to show her willingly.
And Joan couldn't help but crave a little bit more of it, and a little
bit more of it willingly. She wanted to know James better. What
made him the man he was. What energized him in the morning.
What he fell asleep dreaming about. At first he had only been a
devilishly handsome rake. But now, when she looked at him, she
saw him with her heart. With her soul. She was tethered to him
in a way she had never been connected to another human. Part of
her wanted to run. Leave the man hanging there. He was a rake,
so she knew she could never have more with him. Moments of
pleasure were all he was willing to offer.

And she didn't want moments. She wanted…forever.

"Joan? I'm not above begging at this point, despite my predic-
ament indicating otherwise." The man was hanging from a tree
with a partially exposed cock, and he could still tease her.

Realizing her delay in assisting him, she started to move in his
direction. "Of course, I'll get you down."

"Watch your step." The cautioning tone of his voice warmed

her, and she proceeded with care. If she wasn't careful, she would read into how he spoke to her. She would read into his teasing and the tone of his voice. She might even read into the half smirks he seemed to only throw her way. But she couldn't be that woman. She was supposed to be smarter. She was supposed to be the one immune to his charms. She plastered a bland look on her face.

Needing to verbalize her options in order to distract her from the matters plaguing her heart, she spoke, "I'm just not quite sure how to get you down from there…Should I try to hold onto you so you swing your feet down and land on them? Or should I just cut the rope and hope for the best? Which is likely you landing on your bottom."

"I don't want to take you down with me, so…as much as it pains me to say it, just cut the rope and let's hope for the best." He offered an optimistically trusting smile.

Not wanting to drag out the inevitable, Joan took the dagger and sliced through the rope.

"Oomph!"

She rushed to his side where he had fallen on his shoulder. It was impossible not to lay her hands on him, as if just through her touch she could heal whatever hurts, bruises, cuts he might have. Drawing near to him, she realized his breeches were still hanging open, so she squeezed her eyes shut.

"Are you all right?" Asking the question with averted eyes, so as not to observe a particular organ that was still freed of his falls, proved difficult. Her knee landed on his forearm.

He cried out in pain. "Arrgh!" At least, she hoped it was his forearm. The girth was too much to be anything else, wasn't it?

Her cheeks were flushed and her eyes were still closed, as she tentatively asked again, "Are you all right?"

"Mmm…yes," he grumbled. "You can open your eyes." Which she did, just in time to see him speaking through gritted teeth and a clenched jaw while rubbing his backside. "I thought you were going to give me a count." His groans ricocheted in her body, as though his pain was hers.

"I'm sorry. I didn't think about that. I've never been in this situation before." She motioned with her arm to the whole situation. Not just rescuing a man from a trap, but also the partially exposed man hanging from said trap now fallen on his side lying like a clump of dirt. And not just that, but also that this was a man she was now curious to see exposed. Never in her life had she speculated so thoroughly regarding the male form. But after being pressed against him and his enticing male form, and finding a rather large amount of pleasure there, she was currently indecently inquisitive.

He groaned again, and Joan felt a heaviness on her conscience. She hadn't meant to drop him like that, and the man was obviously in pain because of her actions. The guilt rolled through her. She wanted to comfort him.

"I'll forgive you. You can make it up to me by massaging the pain away." With one hand still covering his cock, his other hand circled his backside. "Starting here."

And of course he would say something like that. "You're incorrigible."

He chuckled which led to a genuine sounding groan.

"At least you're all right."

"I'll be fine," he said, rolling onto his back. "I just need a second." It looked as though his arms weighed a ton as he slowly lifted his other arm toward his crotch. Tucking himself into his breeches and buttoning them, Joan felt a pang of disappointment.

"How much time do you need before getting up?"

"Just a few more minutes," he said lazily. "Lie here with me."

He dropped his arm outspread on the ground, and for some reason the invitation felt normal, so Joan rested her head on his arm. Together they looked up into the sky, peering past the treetops.

"Are you comfortable?" Joan shifted in surprise at his question. He was the one who had just fallen out of a tree, yet he was checking in on her comfort level.

"I'm quite comfortable in your arms—I mean, you're comfortable...erm—your arm is soft. But also strong. With muscles." When had she become a stuttering fool?

James's chuckle rumbled through his ribcage and into her side.

"I'm glad you find comfort in my arms," he said. And then ever so quietly, he added, "Someone should."

Another self-denigrating comment that Joan really wanted to dissect. And now she had the time. "What do you mean by that?"

"Nothing." He started to pull his arm away as if to get up, but her hand flew to his chest, stilling him. Even though they both knew her delicate palm couldn't stop him if he had a will to get up. She didn't want him to leave. This was her chance to get to know him more. She had found a small crack, and she wanted in.

"What do you mean, James? You keep saying things like that."

He blew out a ragged puff of air. "It's hard to believe someone would find comfort in me." The words were said as facts, not in search of pity. Almost as if he didn't want to continue the conversation. Actually, exactly as though he didn't want to pursue this line of questioning.

But Joan was not about to give up. "It's natural to find such comfort in friends and family."

"Is that what we are, friends?" Something in his voice sounded teasing, a touch bitter.

"We're friends," Joan reassured him.

"Friends with a lady...seems a bit...odd to find comfort here," James choked out the words as he bent his outstretched elbow to the sky, thus rolling her slightly to her side to face him.

"If it's uncomfortable for you, you can always find comfort with your family."

What was meant to be an encouraging remark produced a cynical snicker. "Right. My family. The ultimate comforter."

"There you go again, James. What does that mean? What's wrong with your family?"

"Let me see." He tapped his free finger against his chin. "My parents agreed on everything."

"That sounds healthy."

"It would be. If what they agreed upon were reasonable things like what to name their children."

"Didn't they agree on James?"

"Oh, I'm sure they did. Which…I must say is probably one of their only reasonable decisions. It's quite difficult to agree on a name for a child. So I've heard."

"James is a nice name."

"Yes. Strong, too." He winked. "But it's not like they had four girls and chose to name them after warriors."

"I always thought I lucked out with the most normal sounding name."

"Yes…Joan…"

The way her name rolled off of his lips sent a trickle of pleasure down her spine.

"Your sisters' names are obscure."

"That's true. But at least the names are all significant and fierce."

"Quite fierce, I would agree. It's a good thing your parents' eccentricities weren't simply oddities. They could have named you after the months of the year."

"Augusta wouldn't be so bad," Joan said with a smile.

"March?"

She laughed and scrunched her nose. "I have to admit that wouldn't be ideal. But December has a nice ring to it, don't you think?"

And she expected him to just agree. The soft sounds in the name would make a pretty girl's name. But instead of responding, he sat dumbfounded, giving her the most peculiar look.

"You're not joking, are you?" he asked dubiously.

"I'm not, actually. December. It has a nice sound. I could do it. Can you see me hugging my little December?"

James scowled at her.

"That's uncalled for. A mother hugs her daughter no matter her name. Even if you don't like the name, I do." She crossed her arms across her chest. "I'm sure your mother gave you countless hugs, with a nice, likable name such as James."

The weight in the air increased, shifting the energy from playful to somber. She wasn't sure what she said, but there was no denying his heavy reply even though he tried to hide it with levity.

"Let me count how many hugs I received from my mother…"

The sentence hung in the air, and Joan waited thinking he would make another joke. He was always the one teasing and joking around with others. This was the most vulnerable she had seen him, and she wanted more of it. Her heart was soaking up everything about him, even his silence was revealing. So, when he continued to say nothing, no number at all, she acknowledged the pain he didn't.

"I'm sorry," she whispered, placing a hand on his chest. The thumping in his chest resonated through her palm. His heart beat to its own rhythm, yet she knew how to read it. Each beat called to her, telling her of the boy he once was and of the man he had become in spite of his childhood.

"It's nothing. You don't know what you don't have. You can't miss something you never knew."

And since he was confessing, she decided to open up as well. She knew something about pain, and even though her experience with abandonment was entirely different, she could relate. And she wanted to. She wanted her heart to be closer to him. "I'll never know what it's like to have my mother at my wedding. Or hold my children. I miss that, even though I never had it."

"That's different. Your mother sounds loving."

"I'm sure your mother—"

"And before you say you're sure my mother loved me. Let me tell you something. She gave me *The Art of War* as a gift for my eighteenth birthday."

"It's a good book. My favorite in fact—"

"It's the only gift she ever gave me." His words were spoken mechanically. Not passionately. Not woefully. Just stated.

"I'm sorry," Joan repeated, feeling helpless. How could a mother never show affection for her son? And how had this man grown into a protective, carefree, loyal human being despite such neglect?

Joan pushed herself up on her elbow and stared down at his face. He was so handsome. Yet he hid so much pain. He was so kind, yet he harbored so much bitterness. And he was full of passion, despite being raised with none.

His deep ocean-blue eyes. Depths unfathomable. Clear at times. So clear that she could read him easily and communicate effortlessly. As though they had known each other their whole lives. Deep blue eyes that could darken to a squall. Reflective of the inner torment that could easily flood him. He battled himself and the storm, attempting to keep the waters calm.

"You're...incredible," she whispered. It was trite. It expressed next to nothing of all that was overflowing in her heart. But she had to say something. She had to tell him...someone had to tell him...and she recklessly wanted it to be her. He called that out of her, her recklessness. It was unfathomable how he managed to do that without pressuring her in any way. He was incredible.

"You're the only one that thinks—"

She pressed her fingers to his lips. Her heart ached for his pain, and she wanted to give him some strength to hold onto in addition to the resiliency he already possessed. "I'm not the only one that thinks this, James. You have friends that think the world of you. And even if your family never saw it, that doesn't mean it's not there. I'm sorry they were terrible to you. I'm sorry you grew up feeling unloved." And as Joan expressed her empathy for him, her heart broke for the little boy that was never hugged by his mother. The little boy that had taught himself not to love. The little boy that had given up on love altogether. She could see the man that he was—the one he hid so carefully when everything else he did with recklessness. She could see the capacity of his heart. If only he could see it too. Tears began streaming down her cheeks.

James pushed himself up and took her in his arms. "Hush. It's nothing to cry over." He was still being strong for her. It was his past. His pain. And although she was only confronting it now, she knew he was still affected by it all. It was probably the real reason he never wanted to marry or have children. How could she fault him for his apparent choice? It was no real choice at all. If one was never shown love, how could one show love? Yet here he was, holding her. Calming her. Reassuring her that his past didn't signify. But to hell with that, his past was important. It did matter. He needed to know that he mattered.

"If you won't cry," Joan blubbered, "I'll cry for you." She hiccupped. "I'm sorry your mother never hugged you. I'm sorry you never learned how comforting a family could be. I'm sorry they didn't show you love." Indignation gripped her heart. There had never been a place for such anger carved out in her heart, and maybe one day she would feel differently, but in this moment, she found something she had never expected. "I hate them for that."

"It's all in the past. Long gone now. It's not worth your tears." Again, he was soothing her. His tone was like a balm to her wounds, when really it was his pain and she should be consoling him.

Her heart was heavy within her. Her throat ached from holding back her sobs, and her already puffy eyes burned from what tears she had allowed herself to shed.

The emotions were all too much.

She pulled her face away from his chest, furious for him, at him, at his parents. At anyone who could neglect a child for no reason. She threw her arms around his neck, desperate for the truth to sink into him. "*You are* worth my tears, James."

— ⟡ —

CHAPTER SIXTEEN

"In God's name let us go on bravely."
—Joan of Arc

Y OU ARE WORTH *my tears*. He couldn't stop the words from
repeating over and over again in his head. People didn't cry
over him. Sure, some women were disappointed when he didn't
bed them for a second time or when he stopped seeing them
altogether. But no one cried for him like this, as if she knew him
and cared about him. As if she wanted to ease some pain in his
life. A pain he was loath to acknowledge. Surely he was old
enough now to have overcome the drama that was his childhood.

"Are you in pain?" she asked, her hands moving over his
ankle.

That light touch sent a small spasm up his leg, and he wasn't
sure if it was pain or pleasure.

"I'm fine." He needed to say something—anything—to get
her hands off of him. To get her attention off of him.

"You don't look fine. You look pale." While she spoke, she
moved her hands up his leg toward his knee. "Is your knee all
right?"

"Yes," he grunted.

"What about—"

"I wouldn't go any further than that Joan, unless you're looking for an extension to what happened last night."

With a deep blush, gradually she pulled her hands down from

his thigh where she was only a few inches away from his swelling cock.

"Something isn't quite right. You seem strained."

Damn this woman. He was strained. Straining at the seams where his arousal was testing the fabric of his falls. But she was still mumbling to herself, "Must be your other leg then." And then her hands were on his ankle. Intent upon finding his source of pain. Let her look.

It felt nice to have such a gentle caress with no sexual motivation. And while she sought, he thought.

Joan hardly knew him. Her aggregated knowledge consisted of the fact that he was a rake, he was a loyal friend, and he could give her pleasure.

Yet...even as he thought about her, he knew there was something deeper. Something beyond the facts. From their initial attempt at communication, there had been something there enabling them to understand each other. He understood her. What motivated her. How her mind worked. And absurdly, she seemed to have the same abilities where he was concerned.

"We should get back," he said gruffly, not commenting on her tears from earlier. If she wanted to cry, he would let her. But he wasn't going to go any further down that road of emotions with her.

He watched as she ducked her head and wiped the tears from her cheeks. She nodded, with her chin still tucked against her chest. James almost felt a stab of guilt in his chest as he watched her stand up.

Letting her take a few steps, he breathed in relief needing some space from her. Her and all her caring. Yes, he could do with less of that.

With a grumble, he rose to his feet. Pain jolted up his ankle more intensely than he would have predicted, and he knew he wouldn't make it all the way back unassisted.

"Joan." At her name, she turned around with a glimmer of hope, and it was torture for him to say the words, "I need you—"

She rushed toward him.

"—to help me." He pointed down at his foot. "I might have turned my ankle."

"All right. What can I do?"

"I just need to lean on you so that I don't put all my weight on my ankle." He put his arm around her slim but sturdy shoulder. Immediately, warmth flowed into him. Almost like comfort.

They took a few steps together. Knowing he was heavy, he asked her, "Is this all right for you?"

"It's fine," she didn't bother to look up at him at first. But when she did, she looked intently into his eyes and added, "I'm strong enough to carry the weight."

And for the rest of the walk back to the manor, James replayed Joan's words in his head.

WITH A DEEP inhale, Joan stood out on the terrace, needing the chilly air to clear her thoughts. Behind her, the house party was throwing another dance. The music was in full swing. She could still hear soft tones of the instruments and the din of voices. Wanting to block out all the sounds, she took a few steps further from the opening. She hadn't spoken to James since this afternoon. When she saw him enter the ballroom, she feigned ignorance to his arrival and made small talk with her sisters. If they noticed (which in all likelihood they did), at least they didn't say anything.

After a short while, she had seen him take off into the gardens. Probably for a tryst. She had seen the way Lady Whitney was eating him up with her smoldering looks. Joan rolled her eyes as a sharp twinge reverberated through her chest. He was his own man. She had no claim on him. He was permitted to do whatever it was he wanted to do. And being a rake, she was sure she knew what he wanted to do. She just wasn't quite so sure why it vexed her so much.

So she stood staring off into the darkness, where the gardens lay, not looking for James.

Too much had happened in the last day, and she needed to settle the anxiety causing an uproar inside of her.

The kiss with James…that was one event that required her attention.

The conversation after the rescue from the trap…that demanded her consideration.

James was complex. Handsome. Carefree. Loyal. But he buried his pain. Pretended it didn't bother him. She could see through that now, and she was growing attached to him. But he was a rake. How could she be so foolish to allow herself to grow attached to the most unattachable man?

If she could just catch her breath, maybe she could talk herself out of her feelings. After all, what were a few fleeting feelings when her heart was on the line? Her heart. Her future. Her happiness. She could maintain self-control around him. She could conquer her feelings. It wasn't as if they had already taken deep roots within her.

"Nice night, isn't it, Lady Joan?"

She dragged her gaze from the stars to greet the male voice behind her.

"Lord Tamely." Inwardly she groaned at the sight of him. She wanted to be alone. And if not alone, at least not with him. He was a walking fight waiting to happen. He was confrontational and lived without remorse. Yet somehow, because of his powerful family, he was still invited everywhere.

He moved closer to her, blocking her way back inside.

"Have you been out here long?"

Did the man not have anything interesting to say? If he was going to waylay her, shouldn't he have come up with something better than that?

"I just stepped out for some fresh air."

"Might I escort you for a walk in the gardens?" He asked with a smarmy smile.

"I think I shall head back inside now. Thank you."

Lord Tamely put his hand on her arm, and a pulse of anger tore through her. It was not enough to consider drawing her dagger on the man, but if he did anything more, she wouldn't hesitate to reach beyond her pocket and grab the dagger secured on her body. "I didn't mean to intrude on your space. You look as though you have something on your mind." His hand squeezed her arm. It was meant to be a reassuring gesture but it only made bile rise in the back of her throat. "I'm a good listener."

"I'm sure you are. Thank you for the offer."

"Would you like to talk?"

"No, thank you."

He stepped closer to her. So close that she could smell his pungent floral cologne.

Leaning in, he dropped his voice, "Do you need some comfort, Joan?" Hearing her name on his lips made her shudder.

"I said, no." She wanted to get away from him, but his grip had tightened.

From down the few steps into the garden, a new voice announced her name, "Joan."

James. She sighed.

He was making his way up the steps slowly, and when he reached the landing where she was, he extended his hand to her.

"Joan." It was equal parts question and statement. An invitation. But more than that. Almost a claiming.

There was no hesitation on her part. As she moved toward him, she focused on the darkness of his eyes. Nearly black in color, all the blue had been pushed to the perimeters.

She needed to be within his grasp. In his arms. It was a safe place to be. But when he took her hand, he gently guided her behind him while he faced Lord Tamely.

"Did he touch you?" James whispered over his shoulder.

"No," she said, shaking her head even though he couldn't see her.

"Was he bothering you?"

She grasped the back fabric of his coat, unsure of how to answer that question. Lord Tamely had obviously been bothering her, but the unrivaled energy emitting from James indicated he might react too strongly to that answer. His body was surging with heat and even though he was standing completely still, she couldn't help noticing that he was shaking.

"I'm fine," she said to his back.

Lord Tamely couldn't hear the back and forth, but sensing something amiss he decided to try and ease the tension with a chortle.

It was the wrong move.

"Do you find something amusing?" James stiffened as he demanded an answer.

And unfortunately for Lord Tamely, he didn't see the need to cower from James. "Just this whole situation."

"What is so amusing about it?"

"You coming up here as if you need to rescue her from me," he guffawed.

"Just stay away from her," James said.

And then that addlebrain chortled again. "She's not yours to protect."

Joan lost her grip on James's coat as he tore away from her, barreling toward Lord Tamely. "Like hell she isn't."

And she hardly had time to see James's fist fly through the air, smacking into Lord Tamely's face.

BAM!

JAMES COULD NOT remember the last time in his life that he had been that enraged. Perhaps his eighteenth birthday with *the gift*. But even that hadn't been a pure, blinding fury like this. That moment of the past had been anger wrapped in disappointment.

Hurt. Dejection. Up until then, he had always held out hope that maybe if he tried harder, became more, grew up just a little bit, his parents might show even a miniscule amount of affection. But on that day, he abandoned any disillusionment. His parents weren't going to change.

If he wanted anything to change, he needed to change himself. So he closed himself off. Love was no longer an ideal. There was no hope.

And to the outside that might sound tragic. To him, it gave him an unshakable ground on which to place his feet. No one could take that ground from beneath him. If James didn't believe in love and no one gave him love, then no one would be disappointed. It was simple. He wished he had decided upon it earlier. Perhaps then the gift wouldn't have hurt as much as it did.

But he didn't allow himself to live in that anger. Until now.

When James had walked up to see Lord Tamely's hand on Joan, possessiveness stormed his body like an army marching in, securing new territory. And then his actions had mirrored that when he strode up and claimed Joan as his.

Joan. There was something undeniably captivating about her. If he had to put words to it, he would call it her loyalty. She was observant, caring, and passionate. Everything his parents had never been. Everything that had been missing in his life, she was it. And he wanted her desperately.

And it was terrifying.

That unshakable ground he had been standing on, riding on, mocking even…it was shaking now. Joan was showing him that love just might exist. And after living so many years ignoring it, James wasn't sure how to accept its presence.

Was it enough that it was a real person displaying it? A real person who looked him in the eyes? Someone he could touch and someone whose touch he could feel to his soul. Was it enough that she spoke to him as a friend? Their conversations easy and engaging. Was it enough that she responded to him? His body, his touch. She allowed him to influence her. He knew she was cautious, yet ever since he had known her, she had been willing to add a dose of recklessness to her days. And look where that had gotten her? Nearly ruination.

And he could be to blame, save the fact that no one saw them together. But that fact didn't signify. He didn't care that no one had seen them together. He knew what they had done. He knew he…what? How did he feel about her?

Seeing her in such close proximity to Lord Tamely lit a fire inside of him that he knew could only be doused if he knocked the man out. There was no other course of action. Even still, he had tried to maintain his composure. But when the man had challenged James's claim on Joan, that was the last straw. He didn't take too kindly to the man's skepticism.

If anyone could protect Joan, it was James. He was a duke. His name and status alone would be enough to protect.

But that thought felt hollow. James wanted to offer Joan so much more than just his name.

CHAPTER SEVENTEEN

*"I am not afraid of storms, for I am learning how to sail
my ship."*
—Joan of Arc

JOAN COULDN'T SWALLOW with the dryness in her throat. Lord
Tamely lay flat on the terrace while James was shaking out his
hand after his right hook to the man's jaw.

Everything around her was spinning. The man on his back.
The man in front of her. Turning. Slowly. There were two of
James. Why were they two? Darkness was creeping in from the
sides and from up above.

And as the world swirled before her, his words churned in her
mind. *Like hell, she isn't.* She wasn't his to protect, yet he had
claimed her. But he was a rake. An ever-darkening rake.

"Joan?" his rakish voice sounded fuzzy. "Joan." Wait. That
one sounded panicky.

Darkness.

Only darkness.

"Joan?" It was little more than a whisper this time. She shifted
her heavy limbs.

Unsure of how much time had passed between her swooning
and her resting snuggly in his arms, she gradually opened her
eyes. He was sitting with his back against the balustrade and her
head was cradled against his chest. His arms were wrapped
around her, one around her back and one pressed gently against

the side of her head, keeping her in place.

When her eyes finally cleared and she could see his face, she was greeted by something she hadn't really seen in his eyes. Concern. He was staring back at her as if she mattered. To him. Of course it only mattered that she hadn't been hurt. She had just swooned, after all.

"Are you all right?" But even his voice was laden with alarm.

"I'm fine," she murmured, not sure that she believed the words herself. Her body felt like a sack of sand. It was hard to move, and she didn't really want to move. Resting against his chest, she felt cozy wrapped in his cologne marked with traces of spice and something distinctly James.

"You can rest here as long as you need," he said gently as his hand brushed along her hair. It was exactly what she wanted to hear. She started to relax, and warm, as he soothed her with his hand. Closing her eyes, she allowed herself to revel in the touch of his fingers slowly tracing her ear, her jaw, down her neck, and back up to her hair.

"So you're not just a rake then, are you James?" It was time to confront him on the airs he put up.

"It's what everyone knows about me. It's what I am."

She reached up a finger to his jaw, trailing along the short stubble. "I don't think that's all you are. There's more to you. I have seen it."

"Perhaps," was all he said. But she saw how his mouth curled up and his eyes softened before she closed her eyes again and laid her head back against his beating heart. A heart she knew. A heart she was sure she had fallen for.

And she was almost perfectly relaxed when her name, uttered on more than one tongue and with varying tones, rang out into the darkness.

She bolted upright, but in her frenzy, her elbow connected with the member between his legs. James shot forward to cradle himself and wrapped her up closer to his chest to make room for his hand to cup himself between his legs.

Terrified to look up and determine who discovered them in this compromising situation, Joan slowly turned her head.

Her two sisters stood front and center. Nobi's hand was covering her mouth. Mimi was grinning to the high heavens.

And if it had only been those two, Joan would have sighed in relief. Her sisters could catch her in the most scandalous of situations and still be trusted not to gossip.

Alas, it was not just her sisters standing there. Flanking them were Countess Linsgate and her daughter, Simone. Both women who could be counted on to spread all shapes and sizes of gossip.

This was not good. This was not even a little all right. This was completely and utterly disastrous.

"I can explain," Joan rushed to say. But then she stopped, realizing she had no explanation for what their eyes were taking in. Lord Tamely lay on the ground a few yards away from them, still out cold. And she was canoodling in James's lap. How could she explain this? She could not.

James's body had stiffened slightly, but his head was resting against the column and his hand was still brushing along her skin, down her upper arm. She only wished the soft strokes were as soothing as before.

His tone was cavalier when he spoke. "Good news ladies. I have heard from the Earl of Dalhone. Joan and I are to be married."

Oh no, oh no, oh no. This was even more horrendous than utterly disastrous. She knew what he was doing. He was caught in this situation, and he was too much of a gentleman to let her ruin herself. He was going to ask her father to marry her. Even though he was speaking in the past tense, obviously he hadn't already made the request to her father. He was just trying to make it look like less of a scandal than it was.

James gently lifted her off of his lap and rose to stand, offering his hand to her in the process. She stood by his side, hand in hand.

"May I present my betrothed?" James announced to the stunned witnesses.

"What happened to Lord Tamely?" Mimi asked about the now-groaning man. Ostensibly all five women were too shocked to reply directly to the proclamation. James had never been considered an eligible bachelor.

"Ah yes..." James scratched his chin. "He didn't realize she was already mine. So I made sure he knew."

Joan's head was swirling again. She thought she might swoon for a second time. Instead, she gripped James's forearm, looking for something solid to stabilize herself. *She was already his?* She knew he was just saying that. It was a story. It was a hefty bounder if there ever was one, yet her heart flipped at the words. And then, just as quickly as it had flipped, it flopped back down. She needed to get a hold of herself. Get this situation under control. Rein in her emotions. Quiet the threats around her.

And if her heart wasn't thumping so loudly in her chest, and her ears weren't roaring with sound, she might be able to play along with James's plan. They could fake an engagement and then call it off later. But her heart...that persistently traitorous organ...it would not be silenced. If this had happened a few days ago, she might have agreed to this plan. But not now. Not after they had schemed together—and successfully, at that. Not after they had kissed. Shared about themselves and their pasts. Not after she had rescued him. And come to think of it, not after he had sacrificed himself and rescued her from the sinking boat. No. Not after all that. It was too much. Her heart was in it. Flip-flipping all over the place. For him.

She wouldn't take him like this. Forced.

She couldn't pretend something now. She wouldn't. Not for him. Not for anyone. Joan was always the one to go along to get along. She never rocked the boat, and she always lived cautiously. Then James had entered her life and taught her that some recklessness added spice to her life, and she was enjoying it. Well, she wanted to live her life for herself. Not as a caged animal, chained to someone for life because of a silly misunderstanding.

She would not accept a pity proposal. Nor would she accede

to a life that would lead to a resentful husband. No. Her future was hers alone. Even if she had to live it that way…unmarried. She knew this scandal could cost her a husband, permanently. But she would always have her sisters. She would not yield to this decision.

So she did something that she would have never predicted, knowing how hurtful it would be. She forced herself to produce a small chuckle. It sounded contrived to herself, she could only hope that it sounded real to everyone else. After the chuckle, she took a step to the side. "He jests." She swatted his arm for good measure. "He's a notorious rake. He knows nothing of love. I could never marry him."

And then, she saw it. She hadn't meant to catch his eye because she was terrified of what she might find there, but she caught it all the same. A flicker of pain. Disbelief. Anger. But it was a whisper riding atop the wind because then it was gone. Vanished into the night.

And so were any hopes she had of knowing him better. Perhaps knowing him at all.

The loss of that potential future almost broke her. She almost reached out to take his hand and retract her words saying, *I'm the one who jests. Of course I'll marry you.*

Her eyes slipped to his chest. Watched his breaths transition from deep to shallow. And when he huffed, it was as if she could see him displacing any honorable notions he had toward her. In their place, he inhaled a new resolve. To accept her decision. To respect her (she hoped). To leave her alone.

And Joan wasn't even thinking about the scandal that would ensue as Countess Linsgate clicked her tongue and removed her daughter from the terrace, so as not to be sullied. Joan wasn't preparing herself for the onslaught of gossip that was sure to follow immediately upon her reentering the ballroom.

No.

She was bracing herself for a future in which she would never scheme with James again. Never feel his touch. His light, warm whisper against her ear. Never kiss him again.

But it was for the best.

He didn't want to marry, and she wouldn't force him to.

It was for the best. She repeated to herself, this time letting it sink into her mind in hopes of accepting it.

After the mother-daughter duo exited, James turned to her.

"Joan, I understand this is overwhelming to grasp in the moment." He grabbed the back of his neck and closed his eyes for a long blink. It looked like regret. It looked as though he was trying to erase a memory from his mind. "But I think it's best that we—"

"I cannot marry you, James." There. She said it again. It was difficult to push the words through her uncooperative lips and against her conflicting thoughts, but she had to do it. James was willing to rescue her again, sacrifice himself and the future of bachelorhood that he wanted. She wouldn't allow it. She didn't need rescuing. She could live this life on her own. And on her own terms. If she was destined to be a blade-wielding spinster, so be it. Perhaps this was the undivided focus she needed to commit to her blade commissions.

She stole a glance at Nobi and Mimi, surprisingly not saying anything, just staring at her. If this decision damned the duke dare, so be it.

She swallowed.

That was harder for her to accept. She cherished her sisters and didn't want to upset them. And surely, this would upset them, making herself ineligible to marry, therefore nulling her participation in the duke dare. Her scandal would sully their reputations as well. But sadly, this decision couldn't be about them. This was the one time that Joan was acting recklessly and completely for herself. The mixture of emotions dousing her as the aftermath of her decision started to settle was vexing. She thought she would have peace if she were to make the best decisions for herself.

James lightly held her upper arms and peered into her face. "Joan, think about the scandal. Think about your future. You will have no offers for marriage. Take my hand. I'm doing the honorable thing. Let me."

"I cannot." She gazed up at him for one last minute, memorizing his face. He seemed to be doing the same, scanning her face. Searching for answers that she couldn't give him. He didn't truly want her. If he did, he would have said that. It was the perfect opportunity to have changed his mind about marriage and love. But he had said nothing. It was patently clear that nothing had changed inside of his heart. A heart that she knew she loved. She hoped could love her. But apparently could not. He was nothing she had wanted, yet had turned into everything she needed. Even still, he would never feel the same about her.

When she looked away, she whispered, "Please go."

And to her profound dismay, he did.

CHAPTER EIGHTEEN

*"The greatest battles in life are fought with a burning
passion within."*
—Joan of Arc

Two Days Later

JAMES SAT IN White's for the second evening in a row, drinking
away…something. He didn't reference it as sorrows, though
some might.

Since the house party, and *the incident,* he wasn't able to shake
a sense of ennui. Dread. Gossip was already starting to spread,
and James hated that he could do nothing to ease Joan's pain. For
surely she was experiencing a deluge of depressing emotions.

"What are you drinking?" Sam clapped him on the shoulder.

James held up his glass. "Open your eyes, and you'll see that
it's whiskey."

"Ooooh, the duke is snarling tonight." Sam plunked himself
down in the seat beside James while Chris took the other side of
him.

"I'm not snarling," James growled. *See? Not snarling.* He patted himself on the back. "What are you two doing here?"

"It's our club, isn't it?" Sam volleyed.

"Care for a game of piquet?" Chris asked while tapping a deck
of cards.

"That's the absolute last thing I feel like doing tonight," he
snarled. *Damn it.*

"Fine." And James thought Chris was going to sit back and

stay quiet. Like he usually did. But he didn't. He sat on the edge of his seat and narrowed his gaze at James. Then he reached over and grabbed James's collar, pulling him forward so that they were eye to eye. "But if you think that for one second I'm going to sit back and let you destroy your life, you're wrong. I will not be a passive participant in this asinine behavior."

James struggled to free himself, but Chris held him tight. "What the devil is wrong with you, Chris?"

"Me?" Chris, the quiet one, threw his head back and barked out a laugh. "You're an absolute idiot, James. And I'll not let you sink to my—to this level. You love her."

"Who?" At this point it was ridiculous to play dumb, but James did it anyway.

"Don't." Chris shook him. "Don't mess up your whole sodding life, you bastard."

"Whoa—" Sam cut in.

"I'm not finished." Chris glared at him. "This ass of a man better step up and do something to win her back, or we are going to be nursing his wounded heart—no, his broken heart—for the rest of our lives."

That shut Sam up. For a minute. Then he looked at James and clamped his large palm on his shoulder. "Chris is right, James. You need to do something. We've seen how you are with Joan." James felt Sam's grip tightening, as if to force the truth into his thick skin. "She's the one for you."

James felt as though he was floundering. He felt something for Joan. Not that he would call it love. No. Love still didn't exist. But she had brought a warmth into his life. Holding her on the dance floor. Laying next to her. Feeling her skin on his. Kissing her. Coming with her. He wanted more. More of her and none of anyone else. And that...well, that was new.

But he couldn't admit it. She had already rejected him. And he knew enough about rejection to appreciate that the earlier one accepted it and moved on, the better one was. Just as he had learned from his own parents. The ones who were supposed to love him the most. They had rejected him. In a despondent, numbing way. And it took eighteen years for him to accept it. Once he had accepted it, he could finally move on. To hell with them. He didn't need them. He was his own man and always would be. He didn't belong to anybody.

And now Joan had rejected him too. And it didn't matter. She didn't matter.

Except she did.

But he couldn't admit that.

He had one last defense. It was ludicrous. He knew. But it was the only one he had, and he was clinging to it with every ounce of strength he had.

"I don't even know if she has a mole in the shape of a moon on her bottom." Yes. There. He said it. Was it absolutely ludicrous? More so than he could have imagined. But it was out in the universe now.

Sam cocked an eyebrow. "What are you talking about?" He turned to Chris. "Has he had more to drink than we thought? Maybe we should sober him up and address this tomorrow. Not sure anything is getting through."

Chris shook his head. "Wait. You're telling me that the chit wants to name her daughter December?"

James shrugged his shoulders. "She's not opposed. She said it has a nice ring to it."

"And—"

"What—" Sam tried to interrupt, but Chris wasn't having it. He shot a stern look to Sam.

"And"—he emphasized the word heavily—"and she kissed your eye?"

James shrugged again. "It was an accident. Her lips landed on my eye when I fell out of the boat."

Chris was shooting daggers out of his eyes at James now. In fact, James was pretty sure he could see a twitch in Chris's eyebrow. And yes, that was a definite tick in his jaw. "So to recap, December is in and she kissed your eye, but"—he held up his hand, as if to brace himself against the air—"but because you don't know if she has a moon mole you—"

"On her bottom," James added. Not sure why he decided to clarify that.

"So because you don't know if she has a moon mole *on her bottom*, you're not going to go after her."

All right. Hearing it back like that, James could really hear the idiocy. But he would not admit that now. He was too far in it.

"You're out of your ruddy mind, James," Sam spoke quietly.

But Chris, no, Chris did not speak quietly. He loosened his grip on James's shirt, and just when James thought his quiet friend was finally going to sit back quietly, he walloped him on the side of the head.

Glasses clinked and the din of the room ceased. Chris took no notice. Thankfully, Sam did. He jumped to his feet and laughingly announced, "Just lost a bet. Nothing to see here."

With some skeptical looks, the crowds went back to their respective conversations, chalking the rude and callous gesture up to more of the men's antics.

"Wake up, James. Go after the girl you love."

"Love doesn't exist—"

"Don't. Don't you dare go down that road again thinking love doesn't exist. Just stop and reconsider how to label that warmth you feel in your heart. Stop talking, James. You don't even have to confess it to us, even though we are your oldest and dearest friends. But you do have to admit it to yourself. This is the last thing I'm going to say to you tonight, don't be a sodding ass. Go get your damn woman."

Two Days Later

THE SWEAT DRIPPED down Joan's back. She wiped her brow in her sleeve.

Bang!

Bang!

Bang!

She clanged her hammer against the fiery blade. It had been far too long since she had been alone in her place of peace.

The clanging sound, the suffocating heat, the power to mold…here was where she always used to find herself.

Another strike. Sparks flew. This was one of many commissioned blades she had received in the last two days, so while her marriage prospects looked dim, her future was not all dark.

This was what she wanted. Work. Rewarding work. Work that she could throw herself into and usually enjoy. Some of the commissions had special requests for names or words to be engraved in them. The one she was most looking forward to was the quote, "In chaos, there is opportunity." It was a paraphrase from *The Art of War*, her favorite book. Though it was bittersweet to think on it, knowing James's connection to the book, she still appreciated the sentiment.

Her life was in chaos. The gossip had spread. She had given up on the duke dare. But out of the darkness came opportunity.

Forwarded through Wes's man of business, Joan had been receiving a number of commissions for blades. It wasn't clear how they knew of her services, and she was quite sure none of them knew her identity, but that's how she wanted it. She wanted to be behind the scenes, doing what she loved.

Clang!

The sound reverberated through her ears. What normally brought her a sense of purpose and accomplishment was decidedly lacking today.

She felt hollow. Perhaps more fitting, she felt like the knife, being struck over and over again. And she couldn't help wondering what shape she was taking from all the blows life's hammer walloped her with.

"Joan." Her name echoed in the small room. When she looked up, she saw Mimi and Nobi standing in front of her, a look of concern in each of their eyes.

Mimi spoke first. "You've been in here for two days. Do you want to talk?"

Clang!

"No."

Clang!

"Joan," Nobi said softly. "Understandably, you're under a significant amount of pressure. Please talk to us."

Clang!

"There's nothing to talk about." She forced the words out. No part of her wanted to discuss everything that was going on. Her emotions were unfocused. Her impulses were out of control. She didn't want to say something she would regret.

Clang!

"If you're not going to talk to us, will you talk to James?" Mimi's voice boomed over all the other sounds in the small space, and at the mention of James's name, Joan stilled.

Was he here? God, he couldn't see her like this. Her hair must be atrocious. She was sweating. The devil she would let him see her like this. But if he were here, what did that mean? Did she want him to be here? No. It was too painful to think about. Her heart cracked at the decision.

The hammering ceased, she placed the tool on the table. Her hands grasped the edges of her apron. "I don't want to see him."

"You don't have to see him. Just read this. It's from him." Mimi extended her hand and held out a missive.

"I-I don't think I'll read it." Joan couldn't help the stutter in her words. It was all too much to think about him. She had spent the last two days driving out the images of his smirking face, deep resonating laugh, and strong arms with each strike of her hammer. Yet she still saw him clear as day. Dark ruffled hair. Deep-ocean eyes. She could still feel his hands on her skin. His kisses on her neck. She wanted him desperately. If only he could want her, too. Love her.

Nobi stepped up, placing a gentle hand on her forearm. "Is it because you don't want to or because you feel as though you can't do it?"

"I just can't do it." Joan sat on the hard floor, and Mimi and Nobi plopped down with her.

"We're here for you, Joan. We can read it together if you want." Nobi's gentle tones washed over her.

"Why is he writing to me?" her voice cracked. "Doesn't he understand how difficult this is?"

"Why is it so difficult?" Nobi pressed.

"Isn't it obvious? The gossip is cruel. It will fade. Of that, I'm sure. But for now, I must go through this darkness. I know I will reach the light. I know I will. It just doesn't feel very bright right now."

Nobi rubbed her back and patted her leg. "You are one of the strongest women I know, Joan. You can get through this."

"I know I can. But then what?"

"Isn't this what you wanted?" Mimi spoke. "You're getting more and more commissions. The more people see your blades, the more business you'll secure. Your dreams are unfolding."

"Not the way I want them to," Joan choked out, feeling foolish. Childish. And ungrateful. But still, didn't she have a right to complain temporarily?

"What's not working out?" Nobi asked.

"I'm alone." She shook her head. "Yes, you're here. But one day you two will be gone. Married. You'll have lives of your own. And I'll be left alone."

"You can live with us—"

"I know. Of course, you would offer that Nobi. Any of you three would take me in. But I would still feel alone."

"We'll find you someone," Nobi said reassuringly. "It'll just take time. I'm sure Wes knows someone. I can even…ask Chris. They're both dukes. I'm sure they would help us find someone willing and suitable for you."

"I don't want just anyone," she huffed. Her exasperation peaking, Joan pulled her legs up and rested her forehead on her knees.

"Why not?" Mimi asked.

"Because I love him."

"James?" Nobi softly asked.

"Yes." Joan heaved a sigh. This was the first time she was admitting it aloud. She loved him. He didn't love her. They had no future. And because of that, her future looked bleak, despite having her business grow.

"You should really read his note then," Mimi prompted.

Slowly Joan brought her head up. "What could he possibly say that would help in this situation?"

"That he loves you," Mimi smirked. Her cavalier response caused Joan to scoff.

"He did not write that."

"He might have," Mimi elaborated. "Perhaps he wrote of his undying love for you and how he plans to whisk you away to elope and then cart you off to the continent for a month's-long honeymoon."

"Doubtful."

"Perhaps he's writing to tell you that he loves you and has secured a special license to marry you anywhere and anytime you want. He's just asking you to pick the time and place."

"Mimi, please—"

"Perhaps he's writing to tell you that he misses you and cannot live another day with you."

"Mimi," Joan ground out. "He hasn't written any of those things."

"You don't know that. And you'll never be sure unless you read his letter." Trust Mimi to spell it out. First the fantasy. Then the reality.

"He might be your duke, Joan," Nobi whispered beside her. "You could be the one that he finally fell for."

It was too much to hope for. It was the impossible. People didn't change. He was a rake and always would be. Joan wanted to toss the letter out. Better not to face being disappointed by him.

"We'll leave you so you can read it on your own," Nobi said quietly but firmly enough that Mimi took the hint.

It was respectful of them to let her have her privacy, so she could decide what to do. If the letter expressed his undying love, of course she would say yes to him. But that was not an imaginable reality. She had seen his eyes on the terrace. Protective? Yes. Caring? Yes. Loving? No. She couldn't bear further disappointment.

Resolved, she threw the letter on the fire.

CHAPTER NINETEEN

"The soul's greatest journey is the path to self-discovery."
—*Joan of Arc*

IMMEDIATE REGRET SLAMMED through her and Joan grabbed her metal tongs to retrieve the letter from the coals.

She tamped it down with a heavy cloth, relieved that it hadn't even had time to char. The paper had only turned a mild shade of brown.

She thought she was strong enough to ignore him. Strong enough to move on and into her future without him.

But her sisters' words echoed in her mind. *You'll never be sure unless you read his letter. You could be the one that he finally fell for.*

It was true. There was hope. And if there was even the tiniest shred of hope left, she needed to examine it.

Waiting for the letter to cool enough for her fingers to open it was the longest few seconds of her life. When she could finally peel open and unfold the letter, she read his words.

Dearest Joan,

I would have sent flowers, but you didn't seem the type. Perhaps I shouldn't be admitting to this, as it discredits the humility behind the gesture, but I couldn't remain silent.

I secured the commission requests and had them forwarded to you. They are better than flowers, are they not? Everyone sends flowers.

Before you get angry and think they are pity commissions, rest assured, I didn't need to convince anyone to make the purchase. I merely showed them one of your blades. Yes, I must confess, I stole one from the house party when I saw you throwing daggers. By the way, seeing your power and accuracy in hitting that bullseye was one of the most impressive things I've ever seen anyone do. And I've seen Sam and Wes compete in an abundance of activities.

At this point, you are probably wondering why I'm writing you a letter (and securing commissions for you).

The truth is that I want you to be happy.

Joan wiped a few tears from her cheeks at his heartfelt words, and then she continued reading.

I never wanted to ruin you. I'll forever feel that it is my fault. I wish you would let me fix it, but I understand your reasoning.

I had hoped that we could be happy together in a marriage. But if you don't envision that, I'll not force you into something you'll resent later.

Your happiness is important to me. I thought I could prioritize it above my own, but apparently I'm a weak man.

So, now, the reason for this letter. Will you meet with me?

Shocked, Joan let the missive drop to the table. He wanted to meet. What could he possibly have to say to her in person that he couldn't say in a letter? It would be awkward to be alone with him lacking a clear objective.

But then again, they had kissed. Where had the scheming been while his hands roamed her body and her legs had straddled his waist? A shiver laced itself up her spine. And all their side conversations that introduced layers to him she had never expected. His family. His mother. Lacking affection. The vulnerability he shared. There was no ulterior motive in those conversations. There was only connection. Pure. Deep. A threading between her heart and his that was still tugging on her.

Glancing down at his suggested meeting place and time, she knew she would go. He was making it easy enough on her that she had no excuse. She had to meet him. At the very least, she wanted to thank him in person for helping her grow her business. And she knew just how she would thank him. The thought brought a smile to her face.

And if that were all that she did, it would be enough. She would have a clear conscience to face her future knowing she and James could be friends. Friends. The word tumbled around on her tongue. Friends was good.

But before she accepted friendship as the final status of their relationship, she had to give them one more shot.

JAMES DIDN'T SEEM to notice his incessantly tapping toe, but if he had asked the lawn, it surely, and sorely, noticed. But who was talking to the lawn? Not James. He wasn't practicing his speech aloud. Mumbling through the words and stumbling over the newfangled emotions traipsing about his heart. No, not him.

And that certainly wasn't him heaving a sigh, huffing out a breath, clasping his hands overheard in hopes of getting more air into his lungs.

It was a hot day, but not so hot as to warrant the trickling of sweat down his back. And across his upper lip. For the thirty-third time that afternoon, he dragged a hand down his face wiping away the excess moisture.

And he waited. Staring off at the hills hiding Bellator Manor in the distance. Joan's place of residence.

He didn't want to give her any reason not to meet him, yet he wanted to give her a choice. So he instructed her to meet him on her own property, on one of the ponds. The plan was to wait for her and if she didn't show up, he would leave, taking that as her final answer. And he wanted to think that if she didn't show up, he would execute his plan. But there was more than a small part of him raging about inside that wasn't too sure he wouldn't just saunter over to her house and force a meeting.

Fortunately, he didn't have to make that decision. There, cresting the hill, was Joan. In a mixture of sage and emerald-green hues that made her effervescent, James's knees felt weak. And he finally did take notice of his tapping toe, which he stilled.

He wanted to run and meet her halfway, but more importantly, he didn't want to scare her off. He was the one who had been scared before. Scared of marriage and a future. Now he was waiting for it with open arms. Literally.

When Joan finally reached him, he could see the trepidation in her eyes. He could feel the invisible wall she had erected around herself, and he hated that she needed to do that to protect herself. But he would share all that with her in time.

No embrace, for now, he greeted her with a soft word, fearing he might break the glass around her. Then, he took her hand and guided them toward a little rowboat.

"We're not actually going in that thing are we?" Joan inquired with a raised brow.

"We are."

"Do I need to remind you of what happened the last time we got in a rowboat together?"

"No reminders necessary. I remember. And this time, I want to do it right." He pulled out an extra pair of stockings from his pocket and waved them in the air.

And then she did exactly as he had predicted, but with so much more impact on his heart than he had imagined.

She laughed. A deep laugh from her belly. The kind of laugh one sometimes waited months for and when it finally did come out, one lingered and drew it out to squeeze every last ounce of pleasure from it.

He laughed right along with her, feeling immediately relieved. No more toe tapping. No more rehearsing lines. He was in the moment with her. The one he wanted to be with. He only hoped he could reassure her of that. He wasn't ready to say that he loved her, but he knew he felt more than just affection. He could convince her that one day love would blossom. At least now he could admit that love probably existed.

Her laugh mesmerized him. Engulfed him. Filling him up to overflowing. And right at the tail end of her laughter, she threw her arms around him.

Stunned, his arms hung at his sides. This was not a passionate embrace. There was no sexual tension being emitted from her. It was pure and simple a hug of appreciation.

She didn't realize what she was doing to him in that moment. James had never felt such physical contact as this.

Appreciation.

Admiration.

Trust.

Respect.

Belonging.

…Love.

James blinked hard at the stinging sensation in his eyes. Just when he thought Joan was done with the hug, she looked up at him.

"Thank you for that, James. I needed that. You are a good man." Tenderness, care, warmth. Her eyes were flooded with gentleness. For him.

Gradually he lifted his arms to pull her in closer to him and rubbed her lower back. "Thank *you*, Joan. You have no idea how much I needed this."

Abandoning the rowboat plan for now, he withdrew his arms and tugged her down to sit on the grass next to him.

"I think we should talk about the night on the terrace." They had never really spoken about it, and it was time. After the kiss, he had been shaken to his core. But he could hardly admit that to himself, never mind explore those feelings by sharing them with Joan. Broaching the subject with her now was risky, but it was a necessary risk. His legs were trembling, and he was thankful to be sitting on the grass. It was grounding him. Reminding him that even though the stakes felt too high, the earth would still be here if she rejected him. The world would keep turning. The sun would keep rising. The grass would keep growing. He took a deep inhalation and exhaled, looking for peace.

"All is forgotten, James. There's no need to discuss it."

"All the same, I want to share my perspective with you." She may not see the need, but he did. In some ways he was surprised that she didn't want to talk about it. And he wasn't sure if it was due to nerves, discomfort, propriety, or really that she didn't care. He hoped it wasn't the latter.

"There's no need—"

"Please, Joan." He would beg if he had to. It was imperative that he explore these feelings with her.

"I'm listening," she conceded as she began playing with the grass between them.

"At first, when we were around each other, we had a purpose. A common objective. It was amusing to converse with you and learn about how your mind worked. Somehow, we were able to communicate with each other so easily."

He watched as Joan nodded her head.

"Then, that night in the garden. When we kissed"—he saw the blush in her cheeks and felt a flutter in his own stomach—"something changed. For me. I don't know about you…"

"Something changed for me too," she agreed quietly, still not looking directly at him.

"Altogether, I have witnessed your power with a blade, your camaraderie with your sisters, your intelligence in scheming, and your recklessness around me."

"I'm not reckless," she defended with a quick glance but then returned her eyes to the soft green blades.

"Perhaps I bring out the best in you, then," he teased, hoping to catch her eye.

But her reply consisted of a mumbled, "Perhaps."

"But the candle was extinguished when I saw Lord Tamely's

hands on you. I saw black. Blackness for him. I wanted to call him out. But I also didn't want to make it something that it wasn't. The last straw was when he challenged my protection of you."

James reached out and slipped Joan's hand in his. He couldn't believe he was doing this, but now was the time. This was the moment to step up and be a man. To go after what he wanted. To open himself up to being hurt in the hopes of gaining what he needed.

"This didn't come about the way I expected it to. Hell, that's mostly because I never would have predicted this. You. Joan. But somehow you've made me believe in love. You have shown it to me. There's something I feel when I look into your eyes. Talk to you. Listen to you. I want to know everything about you, and I want to share everything about myself with you. I want you to be mine. I want a future with you."

"What are you saying, James?"

"I'm saying," he paused, rubbing his thumb back and forth over her knuckles, "you are power, intelligence, and beauty combined. I never thought a woman like you could exist. And then we found each other. You are loyal. You love your friends and family fiercely, wanting only the best for them. But you also know when to stand up for yourself and live your life fully."

He brushed a lock of hair behind her ears. "You make me happy. When you hugged me just now, I knew without a doubt that I'm supposed to be here. We're supposed to be together. I'm saying…I can't believe I'm saying it, but I know it's true." James's heart beat rapidly in his chest. Like a growling tiger knowing he had been captive for too long, wanting to be free. Wanting to love. And be loved. He was taking a chance and risking it all on Joan. If she rejected him, he wasn't sure he could ever let himself love again. But this tiger, his heart, needed to be free to live and roam and be fully alive.

So James did the most reckless thing he had ever done. He opened himself up to an unrestrained future. "I love you, Joan. Will you marry me?"

CHAPTER TWENTY

"Love is the most powerful force in the world."
—*Joan of Arc*

TO SAY SHE was shocked was putting it mildly. He loved her? He wanted to marry her? Not just protect her from the scandal? It was too good to be true. Therefore, it couldn't be true. Maybe he was lying to her? Exaggerating the truth? Hyperbolizing his feelings? When she thought about him, his deep-blue eyes, casual demeanor, but caring soul, she knew he had the capacity to love. But how could she be sure he loved her? And so suddenly.

"How do you know you love me?" Joan asked with caution.

He ran his hand through his hair before he looked up and answered her. "I haven't been with a woman since we started talking. Wait. Before you say anything to that, yes, that is a long time for me. And yes, there is always an opportunity for me to take a woman to bed. But since being around you, I haven't even looked at another woman. I don't want anyone else. I didn't realize it until we kissed. And then we had the incident with Lord Tamely. When his hand was on you, all I could think was *mine*. I didn't want anyone else to have you. I wanted you. I wanted to protect you. Want to protect you."

"I don't know what to say." Joan's heart flapped wildly in her chest, but still, she couldn't say yes to him yet.

"I see hesitation. Tell me what's stopping you." The words were curious, but his tone was demanding. Desperate.

And she knew she needed to be honest. If nothing else, they had been honest with each other, good communicators for the most part. She shouldn't hold back now. "You're a rake," she finally said and instantly regretted as she watched his face fall.

He held her hands in his, sincere eyes pleading with hers. "That part of my life is over. If we marry—when we marry—I'll be faithful to you. You are the only woman for me."

She knew it to be true. Even saying he was a rake now had felt wrong. She had seen anything but a rake over the last several days.

"I believe you James. I know you are loyal. You put your friends first in your life. I've seen it firsthand. I know you have a good heart."

"Why are you not saying yes then?"

"And I need to tell you something that might change your mind about everything." She shuffled her feet avoiding his eyes.

"Tell me," he coaxed her. "You can tell me anything."

With a deep sigh, Joan said, "I've been harboring a secret from you."

She watched as his brows furrowed into deep creases and he clenched his jaw.

"What kind of secret?"

"It's about the duke dare."

"What's the duke dare?"

Joan covered her face. "I'm so embarrassed. I don't know if I can tell you."

"Just tell me. It can't be that bad."

"It is…" The words sounded muffled through her fingertips.

Gently, James pried her fingers away from her face. "Tell me, Joan."

"Promise you won't hate me after I tell you. Even if you withdraw your proposal, just promise me we can still be friends."

"Friends? Given how I feel about you, I'm not sure I'll be able to do that—"

"Just promise me, please, James."

He nodded. She wanted to press him for a verbalized promise, but considering the grim look on his face, the nod would have to suffice.

It was easier to say it quickly, so Joan let the words tumble out, "My sisters and I dared each other to pursue a duke this season."

And then she waited.

"And?"

"And?" she mocked. "And I'm a terrible person for attempting to snare you into marriage based solely on the fact that you're a duke. I mean, not that my sisters are terrible people. They're wonderful. But they have noble intentions. Although I suppose I've heard it said that the road to hell is paved with good intentions...never mind that. This is about me. I'm a terrible person."

James threw his head back and laughed.

"It's not funny, James."

He was doubled over now, holding his side.

Finally, he managed to say, "Joan, your innocence is delightful."

"I can be wicked." She wasn't sure why she was advocating for that, but there it was, out in the universe. It was worth it because the gleam in his eye told her he was happy to hear it.

"Yes. I know." He winked.

"Joan, darling,"—her name plus the addition of the affectionate moniker sent a warm breath through her body—"did you try to snare me?"

"Well, I guess not really."

"That's good to hear," he said with a heady smile.

"I'll have you know that if I were intending to snare you, I would have done an excellent job of it."

"You know...come to think of it...without even trying, you did trap me more than once...the boat, the garden, the terrace. You're a right venerable vixen." James tapped his finger on his chin playfully. "And you did ensnare my heart..."

"I did?"

"Yes. That's what I've been saying, Joan. I love you."

"I thought perhaps you were just saying that to get me to marry you."

James laughed. "First of all, yes, I am trying to get you to marry me. But that's because I love you. Second of all, I would never just say those words. I've never even spoken those words aloud to anyone."

"You haven't?"

"Not a soul."

"So it's just me, then?"

"Yes. It's just you, Joan. Only you."

The heat she had been suppressing, the joy she had been tampering down, the hope she had neglected…she let it all out now. She threw her arms around James's neck and let the tears fall.

"I love you, too, James."

His hand rubbed her back in slow circles, as he whispered into her ear the question she was expecting him to ask, "Why do you love me?"

"I love you because you are caring. Brave. Strong. You are loyal. You have a strong moral compass. Don't laugh. It's true. You may have your own sense of right and wrong, but you have one. You can't convince me otherwise."

"I wouldn't even try."

"Good. Because I love you for who you are, James. I want—" She stopped herself, unsure of whether or not she should share her vision of the future with him.

"What is it? What do you want?" He pressed a soft kiss against her neck.

She let him kiss her a few more times until she cupped his face and held her forehead to his. With a whisper, she said, "I want to have children with you, James. I want to show them all the love in the world. You will make the most magnificent father. You will teach them to take chances. Find happiness."

With the pad of her thumb, Joan brushed a small tear falling from the corner of James's eye. "I want to have little Jameses running around."

"And little Joans," his raspy voice added.

She nodded. "Yes. Perhaps even several of them, all together. We will be the happiest family. Full of love and joy."

James squeezed his eyes shut. "Yes. That's what I want with you."

"Show me you love me, James." Joan leaned back on the grass, pulling his face down with her.

"I'll show you every day, darling."

"Show me, now."

His eyes roamed her body, and her breasts heaved in response. She could feel her nipples hardening.

"I want it to be special, darling."

"It is. We just confessed our love for one another. Please. Don't just say it. Show me."

The palm of his hand cupped her jaw. The other brushed a hair behind her ear.

"I cannot deny you what you want."

"Never?"

"Never." He rolled over and hovered over her, elbows on either side of her ears. His head ducked down, and he placed a chaste kiss on her jaw. Then the chasteness disappeared as he continued kissing her. Down her neck. Beneath her ear. Under her chin. Down her collarbone.

"Do you want me to show you how much I love every part of you?"

"Yes, James," she panted. "Every part of me."

He slipped a finger below the bodice of her dress.

"I can see your nipples are hard. Is that for me, darling?"

Pleasure ribboned through her from her core to her breasts. He was controlling her with hardly a touch. Her insides were no longer attentive to her. They listened only to his warm breath, his soft touch, and his words.

Should she be appalled at his crude language? Perhaps, but she was enthralled.

"Yes, it's all for you, James."

"Good. Then I'll thank them for their attentiveness." His tongue swept over her turgid nipple. She cried out.

"Be as loud as you want, Joan. There's no one to hear us." When he licked her nipple again, she moaned an inarticulate sound.

"I do love to make you feral, darling."

"I'm not,"—a ragged breath clunked out of her—"feral."

"I'll have you calling my name and moaning sounds you never knew existed." A soft pinch to her nipple. A swirl around the tip of her nipple. A suck. He pulled her breast into his mouth, gave a little bite. His hand was sliding up her dress, playing like a feather against her skin. Crossing over her knee, dancing along her thigh. Her inner thigh.

She was vibrating with need. With heat. Pulsating with desire. Ache.

Her moans were coming from all directions now.

"Do you like that?"

"All of it, James. All of it. I want you." She was begging, but she didn't even care. Her body was searching for some kind of release, and she knew he was capable of giving it to her. Guiding her to it and perhaps even more.

"You want me, darling? All of me? I'm quite big. Do you think you'll be able to take all of me?"

"Yes," she scream-whispered. "I'm taking all of you, James. I love every part of you."

He unbuttoned his falls, and Joan tipped her head up to watch. She could see his arousal jutting out. He was large. She was completely unconvinced that she could take him inside of her, but she absolutely committed to having all of him.

Despite lying on grass, she felt as though she were swimming. That this wasn't real. That what was about to happen couldn't possibly be happening. He had been a notorious rake, and he was choosing her to spend the rest of his life with.

Women fought over men like this, and all she had done was be herself.

"Are you ready, Joan?"

She nodded, bracing herself for his entrance, and closed her eyes.

James tsked. "Open your eyes darling. Look at me. I want us to see each other's pleasure." As he was speaking, he slipped his finger into her.

"God, you're so wet, Joan. For me." He pulled his finger out of her and sucked on it. "Oh my God, you're delicious. I need to taste more of you."

Joan's body was on fire. Her breasts arched to the sky as his tongue laved at her nub. She could feel his tongue thicken against her, warm tickles shot through her lips. More pleasure ached through her. Then his tongue narrowed and flicked at her pearl.

"James," she shouted, flying off of the grass.

He hummed his elation. "That's what I want to hear, darling."

"James," she whimpered, not knowing what to do with herself. She lowered herself back down and shot her hands into his hair.

"That's right, hold me close. Where do you want me?"

"Just. Like. That." Single-word sentences would have to do.

His hands plunged under her bottom, leveraging her closer to his mouth. His tongue thickened and pressed against her over and over and over.

"Yes. James. Yes!" She screamed. White-hot pleasure ripped through her stealing all her strength. Her body went limp.

"Are you ready for me, Joan?"

"There's more?"

James chuckled. "So much more. But just a bit more today."

She fluttered her eyes open, staring at his cock where the tip was moist. "That's *a bit*?"

"It's the perfect amount for you. If you're ready."

"Yes, James. I want you."

He grabbed the base of his cock and pressed it against her entrance. The tip, where the moisture was, felt cold. But then she felt his heat. His solid heat.

She could feel him pushing into her. An inch.

He groaned and Joan felt her head loll to the side. He was perfection, and she was about to embrace him fully, in the most carnal way.

"More," she pleaded.

"I'll give it all to you, darling." He pushed another inch, letting her body accommodate. She could feel his legs tremble and she knew it was taking all of his willpower to hold back.

"Now, James. I want it all. Don't hold back anymore. I love you." This was the man she loved. That she would never stop loving. His shoulders were large enough to carry many burdens. Protect her. And through it all he was resilient and willing to open up. She loved him for everything that he was, and she knew he loved her. This was true fullness.

He thrust into her to the hilt. She felt his body slam against hers. She cried out his name. Pure pleasure shot through every cell in her body.

"Yes, James. Again."

With a grunt, he slammed into her.

"You're so big, James. I can feel you everywhere inside of me." She moaned at the pleasure pooling inside of her.

"God, Joan, I've never felt anything like this. You're a goddess. Your pussy is magical. It was made for me. I need you."

"Take me." Thrust. "Take me." Thrust. "Take me!" Thrust. She shouted.

Stars swirled around Joan's head as a release tore her open.

James thrust one more time and grunted. His face shone the exact moment of his pleasure, and he was the most beautiful thing she had ever seen in her life. This was her life. Her future. Her love.

Joan turned to face him, half-lidded, she said, "In case it wasn't clear, my answer to your proposal is yes."

EPILOGUE

"WHAT ARE YOU doing?" Joan watched anxiously as James tugged on her frock. Not that it was a particularly important dress, but she wasn't sure she wanted him to rip the lovely fabric.

As if it were the most normal thing in the world to be lifting the hem of her skirts and studying the area around her ankles, James casually answered, "I'm looking for a mole." He didn't even pop his head up to give her a wink. Apparently, he wasn't joking.

"A mole?" Now this should be interesting. What would suddenly prompt him to be looking for such a marker on her skin as a mole?

"Yes." That was all he said. No explanation. No justification. Just more ruffling of her skirts until they were up around her waist. "Please hold these." He shoved the layers of fabric into her waiting hands.

"Why?"

"So I can continue my search." As if that answered the question.

"No, why are you searching for a mole in the first place?" Joan felt herself squirming with slight annoyance. Could the man be any more elusive?

"I forgot to check before." Yes, apparently he could be.

The man was maddening. Still, he offered no reason behind

his actions.

After she had accepted her proposal and they made love on the grass, they went and told the family. Her sisters were excited, and once her father returned home from his travels, she knew he would share in their joy. James had stayed for dinner and then the two of them snuck away to her room for the evening, which is where she stood now with her skirts bunched up in her arms. Feeling, to be honest, a tad exposed, despite the vulnerable state she had been in out in the open air earlier.

"All right, James, but why on earth are you looking for a mole at all?"

"A moon-shaped mole, to be precise. On your bottom."

"James," she demanded. "Are you going to explain yourself or talk in riddles?"

He tapped his chin. "Shall I explain myself? Hmm…Or shall I keep a secret from you?"

Joan dropped her skirts, catching James's head in the movement. He laughed and withdrew his head from between her legs.

Once she had his attention, she crossed her arms and stared at him. "No secrets, James."

"Fine."

"I told the Betting Buddies that the only way I would fall in love is if I met a girl who kissed my eye, likes the name December, and—"

"You did not!" Joan swatted his chest.

James chuckled as he placed his hands around her waist. Heat spread from his hands to her core.

"I did."

"That's ridiculous." Despite his ridiculousness, her hands still found themselves entwining with the hairs at the back of his head.

"You want to know what's really ridiculous?" he smiled up at her.

"What?"

"So far you have filled two out of three of those."

"What happens if you don't find a moon-shaped mole?"

"Nothing."

"Then why bother looking?"

"To satisfy my curiosity." He tapped her nose. "You can save me time and just tell me if I'll find one."

"I could…but I won't." She kissed his lips softly. "I need to know something. I do remember the conversations about names. December is so pretty sounding. But when did I kiss your eye?" Joan racked her brain trying to recall a moment where it might have been mistaken that she kissed his eye. She certainly didn't recall doing any such thing in the gardens or on the grass. Try as she might, she couldn't think of when she would have done that.

"In the boats," he answered smugly.

"The boat?"

"Boats. Plural. I was in one and you were in the other. Just as I went down, crashing into the water, sacrificing myself for you I might add."

"It was a great sacrifice. One I will always treasure."

"And one I would make time and time again. You are mine to protect. Always and forever."

"And that's only one of the reasons I love you." She squeezed him into an embrace.

"And your hugs are just one of the many reasons that I love you." She felt his lips press against her temple and was reminded of how she knew he was the one for her. It was still a bit of a shock to think he loved her. That of all the women he could have chosen, he picked her. Him choosing her made her feel special. She was not just a third daughter looking to belong somewhere, but a woman, who stood out.

"Back to this so-called eye kiss?"

"Yes. Your lips made contact with my eye just before I crashed into the water. Which makes me realize that you made the first move."

"What?"

"Yes." He pulled her arm's length from him, looking into her eyes. She could feel his intensity wrapped in mirth. "Yes, now that I think about it. You were the vixen all along weren't you?" His thumb rubbed her cheek. The tenderness was almost her undoing. But first she needed to set him straight.

"I did not make the first move. And that wasn't a kiss."

"It was a kiss. Your lips touched my eye. Therefore, kiss. And,"—he raised his finger into the air—"if I recall correctly, you were the one who drew my attention to Sally and Jacob first. So yes, you were the initiator this entire time. Perhaps you did a wonderful job snaring a duke after all."

"That is all debatable."

"Sure it is," he said placatingly, with a smirk.

"It is." And she wanted to debate it more, except he was sliding her frock off her shoulders, placing soft kisses against her neck, and down her shoulder.

"Yes, it is."

"It's beginning to sound like you will agree with me no matter what I say right now."

"Yes, I agree," he murmured, giving more kisses. And then adding a few nips back up her neck.

"Are you going to get carried away or are you going to go looking for that mole?"

"I have the time to find that mole later. For now, I'll get carried away into the heavens with my goddess."

About the Author

Eliana Piers, award-winning and international best-selling author, has been writing and singing stories since she was five years old. After feeling inspired by authors like Julia Quinn, Tessa Dare, and Minerva Spencer, Eliana decided to test her quill on the page.

Writing about love and how two people come to connect and share parts of their souls with each other is now an obsession.

It's not worth it if you don't laugh, learn, or love while you're in it.

Eliana lives in Canada where she drinks an iced cap every day.